LINCOLN: FINDING HIS MARK

PJ FIALA

COPYRIGHT

Printed in the United States of America

First published 2018

Fiala, PJ

LINCOLN - FINDING HIS MARK / PJ Fiala

p. cm.

1. Romance—Fiction. 2. Romance—Suspense. 3. Romance - Military

I. Title – Lincoln-Finding His Mark

ISBN-13: 978-1-942618-49-2

I've had so many wonderful people come into my life and I want you all to know how much I appreciate it. From each and every reader who takes the time out of their days to read my stories and leave reviews, thank you.

My beta readers, Terri, Anita, Tessa, Yvonne and Kimberly, ladies thank you so very much for your suggestions, praise and time.
Of course, my editor and proofreader, Marijane Diodati. You rock.

*My **Road Queens**, who have helped me name characters, places, events and keep me going through it all. Especially those of you who helped make Lincoln, the story it is today by naming these characters, businesses and places: **Tammy L. Wallace** named - Black Gold Pawn; **Karen Ashburner** named Sloane, Victor's Assistant; **Ker Heart** named Kara Dean female police officer from Lynyrd Station PD; **Sue Payton** named Jacqueline (Jax) Masters (Dodge's Heroine); **Bev Sten** named Jake Masters , the undercover agent and the wedding venue, Mountain House Inn; **Nicky Ortiz** named the corporate attorney - Walter Goldman; **Terra Oenning** picked Skye's Wedding Dress; **Nicky Ortiz, Shelly Herrera** and **Amy Ball*** picked the Wedding Party Dresses; **Barb Keller** named the mountain the Santarinos have a house on - Ryker Mountain.

Last but not least, my family for the love and sacrifices they have made and continue to make to help me achieve this dream, especially my husband and best friend, Gene. Words can never express how much you mean to me.

And our veterans and current serving members of our armed forces and police and fire departments, thank you ladies and gentlemen for your hard work and sacrifices; it's with gratitude and thankfulness that I mention you in this forward.

LINCOLN

L et's stay in contact, join my newsletter so I can let you know about new releases, sales, promotions and more. https://www. subscribepage.com/pjfialafm

L incoln hit the floor with a thud. The air flew from his lungs, his legs wrapped around the legs of his prey, his arms tightened and bunched as he held the scrawny disheveled man with the putrid breath off his chest.

"You want a piece of me, you big son of a bitch? I ain't scared," his target spat.

Groaning as he heaved the gangly offender from his body, Lincoln rolled and scrambled to his feet. A quick pounce on the man—not just any man, but Jimmie Molder --- the man who'd beat the crap out of his wife, left her for dead, then failed to show up in court. Jimmie yelled as all the breath he had in him whooshed from his lungs. The smell of stale beer and cigarettes, body odor, and bad breath—the worst of all smells—flew into Lincoln's face with that yell. It was damned near enough to make Lincoln let go, but not quite.

Taking just two breaths to regain some of his lost strength, with a grunt he hefted Jimmie from the floor. With a fistful of ripped, grimy T-shirt from Jimmie's back, Lincoln thrust him in front of him and out the door of the bar. His face may have opened the door for him, but Lincoln didn't care right now. The filthy piece of shit hit him in the back of the head with a pool stick, and that girl-fighting bullshit didn't sit well.

Ramming the front of Jimmie's body against his pickup truck, Lincoln held both of his dirty hands together in one of his big fists while he pulled the zip tie from his back pocket with the other hand. Binding him tightly, he lay his forearm across Jimmie's shoulders as he dialed the local PD. Abe, his German shepherd, barked from the backseat, his face pressed against the window. The gap left for him to get some fresh air wasn't enough to get his big head through, but the incessant barking was deafening.

"Yeah, this is Lincoln Winter, and I've got Jimmie Molder tied up in front of the Two Timin' Saloon." Looking at his pup, his simple command, *"Ruhig"* quieted Abe down.

"Great job, Lincoln. Did you want to bring him in, or do you need officers to come and welcome him home themselves?"

"I don't want this filthy slug in my brand new truck, so I'd appreciate it if your finest could escort this snake's belly to jail in style."

Ending the call, and possibly adding a little extra pressure to his mark forced up against the truck, if the groan and mumbling from the lips pressed into his shiny new Ram were an indicator. Hopefully, the cops wouldn't be long in getting here, and he could run his new baby through the car wash to get Jimmie's filth off it. He'd hate for the paint to peel.

Sirens in the distance had him hopeful, but the small crowd now gathered at the front of the bar watching Jimmie's capture worried him just a bit. He couldn't take on more than three or four of these guys if they decided to jump him and help Jimmie, but he was stuck here right now.

Jimmie kicked back at him, catching his shin on the second kick, which caused Lincoln to grab two fistfuls of shirt and throw him to the ground. His face may have hit the pavement on the way down, but he didn't care about that either. Dammit.

Flopping down to sit on Jimmie's feet, he wrapped his hand around the zip tie holding Jimmie's hands together and held him in place. A quick survey of the side of his truck showed some saliva, but no other nasty looking marks. Maybe he'd need to get himself an old beater truck to run these criminals down. He had the money. Shit, money was flowing in from all sides these days. If it wasn't for his friend and partner, Dodge Sager, helping him run bail jumpers, he'd be working damned near twenty-four seven.

When he'd had this idea of partnering with Ford Montgomery and Dodge to form the bounty hunting business he honestly thought they might have a few lean months. But with all of their contacts, they'd found business right away, and sadly, that meant there were seedy characters all over the damned place. Their response to that of late when discussing it has been, "And that's great for business." Their bounty hunting business to be precise.

Now in their fourth month, Ford only focused on lining up their runs, and he and Dodge were on the road hunting the bastards down. Ford had done this for about twenty years prior to their business formation while Dodge had been a state trooper.

Lincoln was first a cop then a detective down in Arkansas where he was from. The move to Lynyrd Station, Indiana had done him a world of good. Sweet little house on the river, Abe at his side. The only thing missing was a sweet, hot wife like Ford had. Only not the pregnant part —not yet, anyway. Ford had gotten Megan pregnant before they got married. He wasn't going to do that. He just wanted someone to spend his free time with. Someone who didn't need fancy-ass dinners, shows, and champagne.

The tires of the police car crunched on the gravel and brought him from his daydream or stupor, whichever it was. Recognizing both officers immediately, he greeted them with a huge smile.

"Evenin', boys. Look what I've got for ya."

Reaching forward and grabbing a handful of greasy hair, he pulled Jimmie's head up for inspection.

Officer Randy St. John knelt in front of Jimmie and chuckled. "Looks like his face has some improvements on it. Got a room for you, Jimmie, and we promise to make sure you get to court, so Lincoln here doesn't have to come looking for you again."

"Fuck you!" Jimmie spat, and both officers laughed.

"We won't, but I'll bet you'll find a fuck buddy once

you get to prison," the second officer, Jerry Robards, teased.

Jerry pulled a sheet of paper from his back pocket and signed it. Handing it over to Lincoln while his partner took over pulling Jimmie to his feet, Lincoln smiled and took his ticket. It was worth two-thousand dollars to the agency and a cool one thousand that went straight to him. It was his fourth ticket this week, and it was only Wednesday.

"Thanks, Jerry. Don't let this piece of shit get away now." He laughed as Jimmie began swearing up a storm while they put him in the back of the police car. Lincoln shook hands with Jerry, waved at Randy, and hopped in his truck, noticing the crowd at the front of the bar had already gone back to drowning their sorry asses in liquor.

#

2

SKYE

Walking from her upstairs office to the main floor, Skye was still impressed with her workplace. She'd worked here a year and a few days and still the elegance of her surroundings gave her a bit of a thrill. Just as she neared the doorway to the sales floor, she heard the front door chime and the receptionist welcome their new guest.

"I'd like to speak to your HR person, please," the deep, throaty voice asked.

Rounding the corner, she stopped briefly taking in the massive man asking to see her. Six-foot-five if she was reading the numbers embedded into the frame of the door correctly, broad, and delicious. His dark hair gleamed where the sun shining in through the windows touched it. Forcing herself to move toward the powerful looking man, her heart beat a bit faster when the receptionist said, "You're in luck, here she comes now." He turned and their eyes locked.

Stunning gray eyes met hers. The only thought that came to mind at that moment was *wow*! Then he took two steps toward her, held his big hand out to shake hers, and smiled. Was it suddenly hot in here? She could swear the temperature rose at least ten degrees.

"Lincoln Winter. Pleased to meet you."

The instant her hand touched his, she felt it. Electricity ran up her arm and then raced through her body at a dizzying speed. Swallowing to moisten her suddenly parched throat, she tried not to sound like a schoolgirl when she replied, "Skye Sommers. Welcome to Limitless."

Their hands remained clasped as they stared into each other's eyes. Her stomach somersaulted and the heat continued to rise. She could feel the burn in her cheeks, and her chest flashed what she assumed was now a bright red.

"How may I help you, Mr. Winter?"

"First, call me Lincoln. Second, I'd like to speak with you privately about one of your employees."

Nodding slightly she replied, "Okay ... Lincoln. Please follow me."

Turning, she waited a beat for him to begin following her, and then continued to the hallway she'd just come from.

Her thoughts raced to and fro. His mere size was impressive, but since she was tall herself at close to five-foot-nine, her head was the same height as his shoulder. But width? He had that in spades. He seemed agile for a man his size, almost graceful. His hair was short with some length at the top, which he kept neat but not business.

Needing to break the silence, she asked, "Are you familiar with Limitless, Mr. ... ah, Lincoln?"

"I can't say that I'm familiar with what you do here,

only that the business is fairly new to town. Please fill me in."

Okay, this she could chat about without feeling awkward. "We've been in business for fifteen years, though our biggest growth year was just two years ago. We've nearly doubled in size since then. We focus our business on art and precious jewelry. We sell art to collectors and lovers of the art. The precious jewelry is usually more for the fine jewelry collector than the average person. We've been fortunate enough to sell some of Elizabeth Taylor's necklaces, acting as an auction house, but we're also a retailer."

She glanced up at him and almost tripped when she saw he stared back. Slowly breathing out to calm herself, she turned the corner to her office and led him inside.

"Very impressive. How long have you been in Lynyrd Station?"

"Ah, we've just been in town a little over a year. That's when I started here as well."

Extending her hand toward a soft tan upholstered chair, she silently invited him to sit as she skirted her desk and sat in her chair.

"Well, the reason I'm here, Ms. Sommers, is that one of your employees failed to show up for court. He's been charged with a hit-and-run which resulted in a fatality, released from jail on a signature bond. That means the bondsman who posted the bond stands to lose his money and he's not happy. So, I'm here to see if you'll help me escort him to court before the bench warrant which was issued for his arrest is acted upon."

Her stomach rolled. "I'll happily help you out. We have strict standards for our employees as our clients are trusting us with valuable merchandise. It's imperative to this company's reputation that we make sure our employees are law-abiding citizens. What's this man's name?"

"Steven Vann."

Her brows furrowed slightly as she tried to recall who he was. She'd hired almost everyone at this company, except those who had come from California with the Santarinos, when they opened this office. Tapping out his name in her database of employees, her brows furrowed again as she saw his name on the employee list as a dock-worker who had started just two months prior. That meant someone else had hired him without going through her. Hitting print on his record, she picked up her phone, and called the loading-dock manager.

"Hi Micah. Would you please ask Steven Vann to come to my office?"

She hung up her phone then turned to face Lincoln. Her heart stopped briefly as she noted how intently he watched her. To his credit he didn't say anything, and she made a mental note to school her features from this point forward. He was obviously observant.

"So, while we wait, tell me about Skye Sommers."

Grateful for a subject she knew, but embarrassed to talk about herself, she gave the briefest of answers. "I was born and raised right here in Lynyrd Station. Left briefly for college and tried enjoying life in Colorado, worked a time there, then life happened, and I decided home is where I needed to be. So, I came back here, found this job, and that's the long and short of it. How about Lincoln Winter's story?"

He laughed and as he spoke she noted just a bit of a Southern accent. Damn, that was sexy too. She tried not to focus on his lips, but it was impossible. They looked soft, and he wore a panty-melting smile. "Not much to tell, I guess. I'm from Arkansas, but I spent a good deal of time in the service, so I'm from all over. Been to Iraq, Afghanistan, Bosnia, Turkey, Germany, and several other places too horrible to mention."

A knock on the door actually startled her. She was so caught up in listening to Lincoln talk and mesmerized by his impossibly long dark lashes, classic jaw, and the way he looked sitting in her office.

"Come in."

"You wanted to see me?"

So this was Steven Vann. A scruffy looking man, thin and reedy. He had thick hair that looked hard to control. He wore jeans and the company gray three-button placket shirt with Limitless International embroidered over the left breast.

Lincoln stood and to say he towered over Steven would be an understatement.

"My name is Lincoln Winter, and I'm here to escort you to court. You missed your hearing yesterday, and your bondsman isn't happy right now. You've got one chance to keep him from losing the twenty-thousand-dollar bond he signed for you."

"But I had to work."

"You won't be working if you're in jail, so you can come with me now, talk to the judge and I assume your attorney, or you'll be looking over your shoulder for a while. Your choice."

Finally speaking up, Skye addressed Steven. "We won't have this behavior here, Steven. Mangus has made it clear that our reputation as individuals and as a company must be above reproach. In fact, it's one of our policies."

The scowl Steven shot back at her almost made her

flinch. Instead, she raised her chin a notch higher and stared right back at him.

"Gotta cuff you, turn around."

Steven turned around, though not after glaring at her a beat longer. She watched spellbound as Lincoln's large hands made quick work of the handcuffs he pulled from his back pocket. Tucking one of his big mitts under Steven Vann's right arm, he turned them both to the door. Twisting his head to lock eyes with her once more, he said, "Thank you for your assistance, Skye."

The thrill that ran through her at the way he said her name sent goose bumps racing down her arms and legs. She stood staring at the back of the door after he left —*they* left—for a few moments. Then a bit of sadness floated over her when she realized she didn't know if she'd ever see him again. She didn't know if he was married, though it was highly doubtful he was single because how could a man like that still be single?

Lightly shaking her head, she went back to work at her computer when the document she'd printed on Steven Vann, still laying on the printer, caught her attention. Pulling it from its resting place, she lay it on her desk. Then decided to run a report on all of the employees within the company to see how many of them had been brought on without going through her. It was worrisome to say the least, since when she was hired, the importance of consistency in all corporate procedures was highly stressed.

Finding three other employees, all hired around the same time, she printed their employee reports. As she looked over the tidbits of information that had been entered into their system, a knock sounded at her door.

Flipping the documents over, she stood when one of her bosses, Mangus Santarino, entered her office.

"I understand you had a bit of excitement this morning."

She smiled. "Not sure if I'd call it excitement, but certainly troubling which I'd like to chat with you about. I noticed that Mr. Vann had been hired without the consistency you'd stressed to me when I started working at Limitless and—"

"Let me interrupt you right there, Skye."

He folded his lean body into the chair across from her desk, the same one Lincoln had vacated about an hour ago. Her mind went there, comparing the two. While Mangus was handsome in the classic sort of way—three-piece business suits, his dark gleaming hair always impeccable, his deep brown eyes shiny and alert --- Lincoln brought something else to the mix. Stormy gray eyes, which against his tanned skin and dark hair, were almost impossible to look away from. His broad shoulders spread across the chair Mangus now sat in and had filled the space completely. And even though both men seemed to hold a quiet confidence, Lincoln's very presence called to her.

Waiting for Mangus to continue, she blinked twice to click her thoughts into their proper place, which was business.

"We don't help law enforcement do their jobs, Skye. If we have an employee or two that Victor has decided to give a second chance, that means *he* needs to deal with their legal issues, not *you*. I hope I make myself clear on this matter."

"So we're a rehab facility now?" She should have bit

her tongue. The spark that just flew from his eyes told her that.

"We're a business, foremost and always. But, there are things that you are not aware of and you don't need to be made aware of. Your job is human resources and other miscellaneous duties as I see fit. For instance, you should be pulling together the final details for our big Limitless Possibilities auction in just under three weeks."

Taking a deep breath and trying not to give in to the irritation at being dismissed, she smiled. "I'm on time and on budget with Limitless Possibilities. The same as the last three events I've managed for Limitless."

Their eyes locked for the briefest of moments and she saw him shutter and lock any emotion behind a stony façade. That's when it hit her. All those times he'd made advances when she couldn't have been less interested. She'd think on it later and always wonder why she couldn't muster up any desire for this handsome man before her. His Italian good looks, wealth, and charm were always front and center, but she never wanted to take it further than a business relationship. But now, she saw it. He was hiding something. Probably many somethings. She was proud of herself now, that she subconsciously did the right thing.

But, what about this other thing? Things she didn't need to be made aware of?

3

BRINGING IN HIS MAN

~

"Congrats again, Lincoln. We're happy you brought Vann in. We weren't sure how we were going to nab him when he's always with the Santarino crew."

Laughing, he slapped Officer St. John on the back. "It was honestly a piece of cake. I just walked in, spoke to the HR person, Skye Sommer called Vann's manager, and he walked right into the office. Simple. Done."

"That's damned impressive. You must have the touch. Either that or you've just pointed yourself out to the Santarino family as someone to watch."

His smile faded as he stopped walking forward with Officer St. John and looked at him. That's when he saw the tightness in St. John's jaw.

"What does that mean?"

Officer Jerry Robards came up to him then, looked him in the eye, and explained in a lowered voice, "Linc, Limitless is a dirty company. The Santorino family is dirty.

They've been showing up on our radar since they came to town a little more than a year ago."

"What? She handed Vann right over and said they don't condone illicit behavior by their employees."

"He was likely handed over to throw us off. Vann was a sacrifice to show themselves as honest." Robards turned to look over his shoulder then motioned to an office with his head. Taking off toward that office, Lincoln followed him in. Robards waited for him at the door and as soon as he entered, the door was silently closed. Robards and Randy St. John shared this cramped office space. It had dull tan painted walls, two metal desks, one on either side of the room, and little for decorating on the walls except for one large picture of an academy graduation which Lincoln assumed was where these two first met.

Getting an uneasy feeling, Lincoln rotated his head to ease the growing stiffness in his shoulders and rubbed his fingers across his nape. Robards then picked up his phone and pushed a button. "Hey, I have Lincoln Winter in here, and it's time to discuss the Santarinos."

Robards pointed to an ugly, pea-green vinyl chair with chrome legs for him to sit in and took a seat himself behind his desk. Lincoln's mind instantly went to hours before and the office of the gorgeous Skye Sommers. Her office reeked of wealth and prominence while these men, who put their lives on the line every day, had ugly utilitarian furniture as old as his mother. And Skye was as expensive looking as her office. From the designer suit she wore to the Jimmy Choos that encased her feet. He'd seen enough of those in his lifetime. Hell, he'd paid for not less than a few pair with his own money, so he knew Jimmy Choos. Her long blonde hair glistened as it moved which screamed expensive products and regular salon visits. But the most impressive part of her was her smile. Her blue eyes, the color of a spring sky, and her soft voice were so sweet and pure he was afraid if he were in her presence much longer he'd be purring like a kitten. And damn, but her scent called to him. Citrusy and fresh.

The door popped open and Detective Rory Richards stepped in, closing the door behind him. Lincoln knew Rory from their military days—they'd served together: Rory, Ford, Dodge, and himself.

"Linc, great to see you man." They shook hands but the tightness of Rory's jaw didn't go unnoticed. He lay a file on the edge of the desk and flipped it open to allow Lincoln to see its contents. He then half-sat on the corner of the desk, one leg firmly planted on the floor. "So, I'll just dive right in. I want to begin by telling you I had intended to call you to request your services. Your background and experience are just what we need for this job." He paused to take a breath and Lincoln struggled to assess the situation. *Job?*

"The Santarino family has been in the art business for around fifteen years. They got into jewelry a few years later, sort of by accident, when they were asked to be the auction house for a wealthy estate. They aren't as prestigious as Sotheby's and never will be, but they learned there's money to be made, and they're beginning to rake it in—unfortunately, not legally."

Flipping pages of the file to large pictures clipped in the back, he pointed to a photo of a large jewel, not set into anything, loose and sparkling for the camera. "This is a rare sixty-four- carat sapphire. It's never been set and worth upward of fifty-eight- million dollars. It went missing late last year."

Flipping the page, he pointed to a picture with glistening emeralds. "These also went missing earlier this year. They were cut by one of the finest jewelers in the business who works for Cartier. Their worth is into the millions."

Flipping to yet another page, a picture of a stunning sapphire necklace set with gleaming diamonds and smaller sapphires in the shape of a heart sparkled from the page. "This necklace, also worth millions, and missing."

Catching onto the theft, he finally found his voice. "Okay. So I'm guessing the Santarinos have something to do with these missing jewels?" His heart felt heavy at what he was learning. Jewel thieves were ruthless, and he may have just gotten himself into a mess.

"All of these pieces went missing en route to the Santarino receiving facility in California. All different shipments, different months, different shippers. The only common denominator is the family. The owners of the jewels have all filed police reports and insurance claims and as you can imagine, the investigations thus far have turned up nothing."

Turning the file to another folder tucked in the back, Rory took a deep breath. The man was a marine through and through. He was built like a brick shithouse, stocky and solid. His shoulders barely fit in the jacket he currently wore. He'd bet his next bounty fee that Rory had to have most of his good clothes custom-made to fit him. He'd had difficulty finding uniforms in the military that fit his strong, solid frame. He was as tough as he was solid in muscle, and the fact that he seemed freaked out by the Santarinos scared the piss out of Lincoln.

"This is the shit that keeps me awake at night, Linc. Those fuckers are dealing in arms." The picture he turned up showed cases of guns on a loading dock all set out for the photo op. "We confiscated these on their way to California across the Mexican border through San Diego. Three traffickers took off, two dead, before we could get any information from them, but our informant who was trying to get inside knew they were headed to the Santarino facility. We had to pull him because he couldn't explain how three ended up dead and two ran and he didn't. We needed that shipment delivered, but a twitchy ATF agent jumped the gun and killed our delivery. They're bringing in arms from South America through Mexico and reshipping to Saudi Arabia, Pakistan, and Iraq. Probably Afghanistan, too, but we're still trying to confirm that. All in all, these guys are bad news."

"Holy fuck." Lincoln stared at the guns. There were dozens of them. All shapes and sizes. ARs broken down into smaller pieces. Pistols of all calibers and rifles. It was staggering. His breathing grew choppy as his anger grew. He could feel a bead of sweat trickle down his back, and he squirmed a bit to hasten its descent. "How are they shipping them overseas?"

"Art and jewels."

Glancing again at the pictures and then at his friend, he shook his head. "Un-fucking-believable."

"Right. The art is mostly legit. But, there have been a few expensive paintings that have gone missing as well. No doubt they're having them painted over and shipping them to Italy or Paris, and from there, they're sent on where they go more unnoticed—in the false bottom of the crates used for shipping weapons. We have a guy in Europe who's inside the Santarino facility in Paris. He's undercover, of course, and he's gathering intel. But not enough for us to shut the operation down. We need to know all the moving pieces and where the Lynyrd Station facility fits in."

Sitting back to relieve his now aching back, he looked up at Rory. "How are you getting all this intel?" Rubbing the back of his neck again he asked, "And are there insurance claims on these paintings too?"

Rory glanced at the two officers who sat very quietly during the whole conversation and they shrugged. "I'm the liaison between this department and the feds. And, yes, there are insurance claims, which is beginning to make the Santarinos twitchy. They haven't been careful enough in their operations. Too many claims around items on the way to their facilities. One of the things that has saved them so far, is that the transportation companies shipping these items to the Santarinos are different. They are likely paid off to keep the trails clean as to the Santarinos, but since we don't have one singular company with more than one lost shipment, we're having some difficulty making the complete connection. But, we're working on it."

Whistling, Lincoln nodded. "Impressive, bro. I mean your being the liaison, this other shit is messed up."

"Not sure how impressive it is. They needed someone here who could keep an eye on things. It didn't hurt that I have the military background and a position within the police department. And, I dated my contact's sister in high school, so there's that."

"It's those connections that you never know what they'll bring." Lincoln glanced again at the picture of the guns, and his jaw tightened. Skye was too good to be true apparently. "So it appears I may have made myself a target?"

"Maybe and maybe not. Now you've made contact with

their HR person. Is she someone who you might be able to schmooze with and see if you can get more intel? Nothing too big, but maybe a name or two? We're of the belief that they're selling guns locally as well as internationally through a local contact. We've uncovered a couple of those missing guns on one or two thugs we've recently arrested. The serial numbers are scratched off the guns, but they seem to be flooding into the area recently and are eerily similar to the ones in this picture right here."

Locking his eyes on the offensive picture again, he leaned forward to get a closer look. Rory pointed to the side of the weapon where the serial number had been scratched off.

"How many of these have you recovered?" His heart felt heavy, yet it also began to race.

"So far, only three. But that's three in a week and we're worried there are more out there."

Lincoln rubbed the back of his neck and stretched his shoulders. "So, you need me to cozy up to Skye Sommers and see if she has any more information?"

Rory laughed. "Already on a first-name basis with her? I've seen her picture, so it shouldn't be a hardship, right?"

"No." He said it too fast and Rory laughed a bit harder.

He leaned forward, the grin still on his face. "Are you enamored?"

"No." He said that too quickly too which earned him another chuckle from all three of the men facing him.

Rory flipped the pages to an earlier one in the file, and there was Skye's picture showing her standing in the gallery of Limitless with a tall, dark-haired man. Her gleaming blonde hair cascaded in waves over her shoulder; her smile was stunning. She wore a light blue suit and heels to match. Her hands were clasped together in front of her and her posture was straight and solid. As he looked a bit closer, he saw that the man had his hand behind her at the angle of her lower back, and when his eyes shifted back to hers, he thought he read uncomfortable on her face.

"She's with Mangus Santarino, one of the Santarino sons. The company is owned by their father, Giovanni, but he isn't around much. Mangus and Victor are here the most, and actually, Victor does more travel back and forth to California than Mangus. Since we aren't low profile as cops, small town and all, we can't get that close. That's where you come in."

"Okay. So just chat her up and see if I can get any information from her? A name of maybe a local contact or business or something?"

"Maybe a drink or a dinner out or something. Get to know her and see what's going on over there."

Right. A drink or a dinner out. That would mean he'd have to put on a suit and uncomfortable shoes. Looking at her, she screamed five-star restaurants and Dom Pérignon —a princess—not beer by the lake and a burger. But since he could afford a fancy dinner and Dom, and she'd be gorgeous to look at for a couple of hours, what could it hurt? His mind raced to the restaurants in Lynyrd Station and where they could go. He hadn't been in town long and not sure of all of the best places to hit. Ford could help him out with that. Ford's nightmare of an ex-wife liked the finer things. Just the thought of Tamra set his spine to tighten and his jaw to clench.

"Linc, you're perfect for the job. Military background. Detective experience. And you've made contact."

Looking closely at his friend, he saw concern. Running

his fingers over his nape, he let out a breath. "I need to talk to Ford and Dodge, Rory. It affects our business."

"Right. When you talk to Ford, tell him the feds will pay. Handsomely. They've moved the priority on this to top twenty. Which, on the surface, doesn't seem like much, but in the overall scheme of all that's going on in the world, that's pretty high."

*

"So, in a matter of a few days we could be looking at a sizable payout and perhaps some contacts for future work. I told Rory I'd need to speak with you guys and we'd get back to him, but he wants to know by this evening."

Dodge sat back on the sofa in Ford's living room, a bottle of beer resting on his knee in one hand and his other hand running his thumb over his bottom lip. Lincoln recognized this motion by now. Dodge was eager but trying to keep his enthusiasm to a minimum, just in case. His sandy hair was still clipped short and it made his green eyes stand out. "Okay, so it'll mean a few things for the business." Sitting forward Dodge locked eyes first with him and then with Ford before continuing. "We'll be short-handed on this side of the business for a while, but I'm game to step up and make more jing. I'd like to finish my game room at the house and I'm itching to pay off mom and dad's house for their anniversary; I'm close. That takes care of the work side of Big Three Bounty Hunting. But, what it means for you Linc, is that you're putting yourself in some real danger. I thought you wanted to get away from that shit."

"I did. I do, but I can't deny I'm both flattered to be asked and interested in being a part of pulling this type of shit off the streets. It's what we'd always talked about, doing good things while using our skills and making a shit-ton of money while doing it."

Ford cleared his throat, "It does sound interesting and I've got to admit, I'd prefer to know the streets aren't being flooded with stolen guns. While we're apprehending these jackoffs out there, we sure don't want to add being shot to the mix. That's already a possibility, but if they have untraceable guns, it may make the average law breaker a bit bolder."

Ford locked eyes with him and they held for a few moments. "Linc, it's your ass on the line, what do you want to do?"

He took a deep breath, leaned forward on the leather chair he sat in at an angle to the sofa and responded. "I'd like to do it. That is if you and Dodge can manage Big Three while I'm working this case. Big Three is my first priority. What do you two think?"

Looking at Dodge he saw the corner of his friend's mouth tip up, he knew his answer. Dodge was already planning how he'd surprise his parents with the clear title to their home. "I'm in. I've got nothing pressing right now except scrubbing the streets of lowlifes."

Both he and Dodge looked at Ford. His answer was to lift his beer bottle in the air, which they each clinked to theirs before downing the remaining beer in their bottles.

Ford then added, "I'll call Rory in the morning and confirm payment and get details."

#

4

LET THE DETECTIVE WORK BEGIN

Leaving Ford's house, Lincoln's mind wandered. First of all, shit! The thought of the striking Skye Sommers being involved in some seriously dirty shit made him sick. But, he needed to do what he could to get those damned guns off the street and to help the feds get these dirty bastards. Now he needed to figure out how to approach Skye, and hopefully, ask her out on a date and see if he could gather some intel from her.

Main Street was fairly empty for a Thursday afternoon. At four o'clock the street was usually full of cars as people stopped at this store or that to pick up items before heading home to make or eat supper. He liked Lynyrd Station as a general rule. Quaint, small town and most folks knew you. When a helping hand was needed, it was there, but most of all what he liked was that he felt welcome. When he first moved to Lynyrd Station, Ford and Megan introduced him to their friends and some of the locals in business and he'd always felt genuinely accepted. It was irritating that the Santarinos were hell-bent on trying to destroy its reputation with their shady bullshit. But hopefully, he'd be able to get them taken down before they were able to do too much damage.

He enjoyed the view along Main Street, his favorite building being the Copper Cup, with its old saloon feel. He and Dodge had shared many a beer there, shooting the shit over a game of pool. In only the four months the agency had been open, they had a plethora of stories to tell about their captures. It was comical, really, some of the shenanigans that went on when one was trying to evade capture.

It didn't look like the place was hopping yet, but maybe in an hour or so he'd be ready to pop in and have a few. Abe whined from the backseat and Lincoln glanced in his rearview mirror to check on his pup. Their eyes locked briefly, then Abe rewarded him with a lick on the cheek. Chuckling, he swiped at his saliva-covered cheek and that's when he saw her. Skye Sommers was getting out of her sweet steel-gray Mustang — a Shelby — if he knew his cars. Though a bit older, it still looked pristine. A quick glance behind him showed no cars, so he slowed his truck, and pulled in behind her. He couldn't help but be captivated by the long legs, made longer by the height of the sleek black Jimmy Choos she wore. Her sexy, tan pencil skirt stopped at her knees, but she'd shed her matching jacket, which was a bonus because the black cami she had on hugged her curves in the most delicious way. He whistled and Abe whimpered once again. "Sorry, buddy," he apologized to his pup, his eyes never leaving the sultry Skye Sommers until she disappeared into the hardware store across the street.

Reaching back, he scratched Abe under the chin and commanded, "*Rohig,*" before exiting his truck.

Entering the hardware store, he sauntered down the first aisle, intending to wander the store and accidentally bump into Skye. Then he heard her voice up front at the register. "Hey Dan, is there any way you can allow my dad an extension on his bill with you?"

Dan, the store owner and genuinely a great man, responded in his usual no-bullshit way. "I can offer a bit more time to get caught up, but can't offer any more credit, Skye."

"Thank you and I understand." The register rang, a bag rustled, and no more sound other than the soft music piped through the store.

Well, what on earth is going on here? She dresses like a million bucks but is asking for credit for her family? Maybe she's a shitty money manager.

Making his way to the front of the store, he saw her back as she left the store with a bag in her hand.

Once again watching her walk across Main Street, his body thrummed with awe of her very demeanor. No doubt the woman was stunning. She opened the door to her Mustang and he was rewarded with an excellent view of her long shapely legs as she pulled them into the car one at a time. Tossing her hair over her shoulder, he heard the muscle car purr to life. She twisted her neck to see if anyone was coming down the street before pulling out, and that's when her eyes lit on his. Her lips tightened before she eased her sleek car from its parking spot and down the street.

Climbing into his truck, he headed in the same direction, hoping to see where she was going and make his move—so to speak.

Not more than a couple of miles out of town he found her car pulled over to the side of the road, steam rolling from under the hood. Pulling up behind her, he watched as Skye exited her car and tried to open the hood without getting burned. She jumped back once, as steam burned her arm.

"Hold on there, let me help you," he yelled so she'd hear him over the hissing of the car. When her eyes landed on him, he was first struck with the thought that she was relieved, then her eyes narrowed, and he could swear she was pissed that it was him coming to her rescue.

"I don't need your help." She rubbed her arm, now reddening from the slight steam burn.

"It appears you do, Skye."

"No, I don't." Reaching into the space between the hood and the car, she quickly released the hood lock and pulled the hood up. The steam billowed out in thick full clouds. Both of them stepped back. It didn't go unnoticed that she refused to look at him, preferring to keep her eyes trained on the steam rolling from her car.

"It just needs to cool a bit, and then I'll add antifreeze to it. I'll be on my way in a minute or two."

"How long has it been acting like this?"

Finally looking at him, her mouth tightened and he could see her shoulders stiffen slightly. "Awhile. It's not a big deal."

"Honey, it could be. If you keep letting it get hot like this it'll destroy your engine, then you're going to have a shit-ton of issues and costs to deal with."

Slamming her hands on her hips, she turned to face him. "It's really none of your business, and why are you following me?"

He turned his body to face her; his eyes captured hers and held firm while he waited for her to relax before continuing. "I'm not following you. I saw you stopped on

Main Street and before I could talk to you all I saw was your back. I wanted to ask you out to dinner."

"Dinner? Really? I don't have time for dinner."

"Looks like you do, sweetheart." He nodded to her car. "We can have a quick dinner and a drink, and by the time we get back here your car will be cooled down and ready to drive."

Her shoulders dropped. "I don't, Lincoln. I'm sorry, but I have ... things I need to do."

Her tone softened, and he felt that was a good sign.

She walked to her car and pulled out the bag she'd carried from the hardware store from the floor of the backseat along with a rag.

He reached forward and gently took the rag and antifreeze from her hands. "Hey, let me help you. You'll get my 'man card' revoked if I let you do this in my presence."

She giggled slightly, and that sound—pure and sweet—shot him in the gut.

"Far be it for me to take away a man's 'man card.'"

Carefully removing the cap from the radiator, he set it alongside the opening and twisted the cap on the antifreeze jug. Slowly pouring it into the radiator, he stood slightly back as the hissing and popping sounded. He could feel her presence next to him, and he was sure if it weren't for the smell of the hot car and antifreeze, he'd be able to smell her citrusy perfume. His stomach curled tightly as he thought about this riot going on between his body and head. He was certainly attracted to her in a physical way. But, his head reminded him that she worked for a company willing to forego laws and human life to make money, and he still didn't know what her place was in all of that.

Finished with the antifreeze, he tightened the cap on

the radiator as well as the empty jug in his hands. He wiped his fingers with the rag she had with her and handed it back to her.

"I can toss the jug when I get home," he offered.

"That's okay. I'll take it. You don't need to toss my garbage."

She gently took the empty plastic container from his hands and their fingers brushed. Her eyes shot to his, and he saw the pulse quicken in her neck. Swallowing, she stepped back and looked at the ground. "Thank you for your help."

He watched her sexy ass sway as she walked to the side of the car and set the container on the floor of the backseat. He reached up and lowered the hood, pushing firmly on it to ensure it latched into place.

Following her to the side of her car where she stood, he asked once again, "Now, what will it take to encourage you to have dinner with me?"

"Lincoln, thank you for helping me, but I honestly can't. I have things ..." She paused and swallowed. "I'd like to, really, but I have about two more hours or so of work to do."

His brows raised, and he saw her bite her bottom lip, indecision clear on her face. "Something I can help with?"

Watching her chest as she inhaled deeply, then exhaled, his body stirred, ignoring his brain. He needed to get this in perspective and stop pushing. Maybe there was another way to gather intel on Limitless. Then she surprised him.

"Why don't you follow me? I'll have dinner with you before I finish my chores." Not waiting for an answer, she quickly sat in her car and the engine purred to life before he could process the change in direction.

Alrighty then. And then he thought, chores?

5

WELCOME TO SOMMER'S DREAMS

Okay, so once again she was in Lincoln's presence. Well, not really, but she would be as soon as they arrived at their destination. And dinner? What on earth was she thinking? She'd gotten her ass chewed out twice today for helping Lincoln Winter. Mangus Santarino came storming into her office hot and bothered because she'd helped the police take Steven Vann into custody. He ranted and raved about how she had no right to do that, and if anyone ever came to the office again looking for a Limitless employee, she was to consult with either him or Victor. Then awhile later, Victor came in and really chewed her ass. He told her if she did anything like that again, she'd find herself sitting on the outside looking in. Here she thought she was doing something good. What a crap today had taken on her lap.

Turning down the country road that led to her parents' home, a quick glance at the passenger seat confirmed that her briefcase was still there. Not that it had anywhere to go, but the contents made her terribly uneasy, and the somersault in her stomach told her she could get into serious trouble for taking the documents from the office. But something compelled her to, and she found it difficult to ignore her thoughts on the subject.

Another quick glance in her rearview mirror told her Lincoln was still following. She swallowed the lump forming in her throat at the thought of spending more time with him. But honestly, it didn't seem as though he was eager to go away, so she may as well show him the predicament she dealt with on a daily basis. Then, maybe he'd realize she's a hot mess and leave her alone.

Trying to allow the serene pastures and country air to bring a peace and calm to her, she inhaled and held her breath for a second before slowly releasing it. The greens were so vibrant, and the smell of fresh cut hay floated in the air. She pushed a button on her armrest to roll her window down. The weather was still warm, even though it was nearing five-thirty. Making the last turn onto her parents' driveway, she glanced around to see if any of the horses they still had were turned out to pasture. Noting only two, she assumed her mother had the other three either in a back pasture or in the barn.

Pulling to a stop at the side of the house, she stepped out of her car and stood alongside it waiting for Lincoln. Leaning her backside against the warm metal, she watched as his very blue pickup rolled to a stop next to her car. As the back window of his truck rolled down, a big German shepherd popped his head out, and his eyes locked onto hers. Her head tilted to the side as she continued to admire the beautiful dog, and he was admirable. He wasn't barking or making a nuisance, but he was assessing her.

"Abe ... *fruend.*" Lincoln's deep, sexy voice floated over to her, and Abe's tail wagged. He looked at her then, and for a brief moment their eyes locked. "It means 'friend.' Do you mind if I let him out to stretch his legs a bit? He won't run, and he won't bother anything."

Straightening up from leaning on her car, she shook her head. "Oh no, of course not."

Stepping back and out of the way so Lincoln could open the door, Abe jumped down and sat still, looking up at Lincoln. Obedient. Waiting for his command.

Lincoln reached into the back and pulled a tennis ball from under the seat. Tossing it across the yard, he commanded, "*Holen.*"

Abe took off after his ball and Lincoln's smile was breathtaking. She admired him for a moment. The dark richness in the color of his hair gleamed in the waning sunlight; his profile was strong and classic. The breadth of his shoulders was impressive, and if she were honest with herself, the whole of him was extraordinary as all get out.

Abe ran back and dropped the ball at Lincoln's feet, then stared up at his master with such adoration in his eyes, she was jealous. He leaned down, patted Abe on the head and said, "*Guter Junge.*" Then he picked up the ball and tossed it again.

Her German was limited but she recalled that *Guter Junge* meant good boy, and she smiled. For a man his size, he was surprisingly gentle with Abe. Allowing her eyes to travel down his forearms, her heart raced a bit faster. What was it about a man's forearms that could be so darned sexy? The dusting of dark hair was appealing in so many ways. She felt him turn slightly toward her and her cheeks flamed red at being caught admiring him.

She cleared her throat. "Welcome to Sommers' Dream, the home of my parents, Jeff and Melissa Sommers."

Watching as he assessed the surroundings, she slightly

cringed at the sad state of things as they were. There wasn't enough money and there weren't enough hours in the day to keep the farm in the condition it had been in before the accident. A testament really to her father, who she'd always believed was a hard worker, but she now knew just how hard.

"So, tell me about the farm. I saw horses when we pulled in. Do your parents raise them or breed them?"

"We used to be one of the best breeding farms in this area, hired by some of the most prestigious racing farms from here to Lexington, Kentucky."

Watching his face as he took in this information, he picked up Abe's ball and tossed it again, then he turned to her and asked, "Why used to be?"

Yeah, here it came and he'd go running for sure. "My father had an accident last year, just after I got my job at Limitless. He was cutting hay out in the backfield and the tractor hit a deep hole, one that we've yet to figure out how it got there. The tractor overturned and his back was broken. It's been a long year of recovery, and he's still nowhere near the end of his healing and rehab. So, I come out after work every day and on the weekends and do what I can for him. Breeding jobs had to be turned down and the farm just isn't what it used to be. I can only do so much. Momma too. She's mostly inside helping my dad."

He nodded but to his credit he refrained from saying that he was sorry. She was so damned sick of people saying that. She knew it was just what they thought should be said, but it had gotten old very fast over the past year.

"Anyway, if you'd like to come in, I'm sure Momma has supper ready, then I'll come out to the barn and get the chores done before dark."

He whistled. "Abe. *Hier.*" His dutiful pup came running. Lincoln opened the door and he jumped right in. Moving to the back of his truck, he opened the tonneau cover, pulled a cold bottle of water from a cooler and a plastic bowl from a duffle bag. He smiled at her as he walked to the backdoor of his truck, opened it, set the bowl on the floor and poured the water in it for Abe to slake his thirst.

"Good boy." Even though drinking his water, Abe's tail wagged. She imagined anytime Lincoln Winter complimented someone they'd wag their imaginary tails. There was a presence about him that made a person want to do good for his praise.

"Sometimes you speak German, sometimes English. Doesn't that confuse him?"

His chuckle came from deep in his chest and it was sexy. "Nope. He's bilingual."

She snickered and began walking to the backdoor of the large, brick two-story home she'd grown up in. "Come on in."

Climbing the three steps to the backdoor, she grasped for the handle, but he was there first, reaching around her to be a gentleman. She caught a whiff of his cologne and her nipples pebbled. If a person could smell masculine and strong, he did.

"Thank you," she whispered because that's about all she could muster.

"Momma. Daddy. I'm here and I brought a friend."

The mud room was well lit and neat and had always been where they entered the house from outside. Lifting her left heel behind her, she pulled her sweet black Jimmy Choo from her foot and tried to hide the grimace she made when the cost of these shoes flew through her mind.

It had been a splurge when she first got her job at Limitless. She'd felt like her life was finally on track again. Landing her dream job, making more money than she ever had. The possibility of being able to travel around the world to the many Limitless facilities and maybe one day, transferring to work at one of them seemed like a fantasy come true. Lynyrd Station would always be home, but seeing some of the world was a childhood dream.

Quickly lifting her right foot and pulling that heel off, she noted Lincoln doing the same. Before she could get the words from her mouth that he didn't have to do that, he winked, neatly set his shoes along the row of others, and stood back waiting for her to precede him into the kitchen.

She smiled at him, and the smile he returned took her breath away. She'd never seen such beauty in a man. While impressively large and strong, his features were mesmerizing. She'd never seen such beautiful gray eyes, and those dark lashes framing them were envious.

"Hi, sweetheart, I made spaghetti tonight. It's just about ready to ..." Her mother turned with a bowl of steaming hot pasta in her hands and froze when her eyes landed on Lincoln.

"Well, hello," her mother said, if not a bit breathless, then certainly with some awe in her voice.

Lincoln chuckled behind her, no doubt used to this reaction from women. She stepped aside and held her hand toward her mother. "Mom, this is Lincoln Winter. Lincoln, my mom, Melissa."

She watched as the bowl of pasta was deposited on the table and her mom swiped her hands on the towel tucked into her jeans as an apron. She met Lincoln in the middle of the room and they shook hands.

"It's nice to meet you, Melissa."

Did her mother just sigh? Shit. She did. She didn't want her mom—or dad, for that matter—getting attached to Lincoln. This was nothing more than showing him what a mess her life was so he'd go on his merry way. Victor and Mangus didn't want her helping him, and she didn't need the complication. She needed the job right now and couldn't risk losing it over a man. Not again.

"Oh ... it's nice meeting you, Lincoln." Yep, she was sighing.

"Momma, where's Daddy?" She needed to get this show moving.

Her mother's lips thinned and her posture straightened. "He's had a very bad day today, and he's in his chair in the living room. I tried helping him up, but I couldn't do it myself. I was waiting for you to help me."

Nodding, she stepped toward the living room, Lincoln and her mother on her heels. "Hi, Daddy."

Her father sat in his burgundy recliner, purchased just after his accident with the lumbar supports he needed during his healing time. Little did any of them know how well it would be used just one year later. He looked up at her, his formerly tall, straight shoulders now slouched from pain and sadness. He hated being so helpless. It gnawed at her gut to see him so defeated.

"Hi, sweetheart. Hope you had a good day today." His voice, which had once been so strong and deep, now sounded hollow and detached.

"It was good, Daddy. I'd like to introduce you to Lincoln Winter." She turned to Lincoln. "My dad, Jeff."

Lincoln leaned forward with his hand out and took Jeff's hand in his. They shook hands, and she watched her father's face light up just a bit as they engaged in some silent man speak. "I understand today was a bad day and you need some help. Allow me to be of assistance."

Lincoln took charge and leaned down in front of her father, wrapped his arms around her father's hips and slowly pulled him to the front edge of the recliner. Once he had him in place, he said to her dad, "Fast or slow?"

"Fast."

She shot a quick glance at her mother whose brows now furrowed as she watched Lincoln make quick work of a task they would have taken fifteen minutes to complete.

Bending his knees before her father, she watched as her dad's arms wrapped around Lincoln's shoulders and in just a few seconds, Lincoln stood with her father in front of him. Giving her father a moment to get his bearings, he waited until he nodded and removed his arms.

Her father's hands gripped the walker her mother set in front of him, and she saw him smile just a bit.

"If you ladies want to head on in to the kitchen, I'll make sure Jeff gets in okay."

They both hesitated until Lincoln nodded at her, then he winked again. Didn't that just wing through her body and straight to places that should be left out of this whole scenario?

She nodded to her mother who walked ahead of her to the kitchen. Behind her, she heard her father saying, "I love them, but they hover too much."

"That's what women do," Lincoln responded. She fought the urge to turn and look at him. Then she heard, "But they're gorgeous, and that's a plus."

Her father chuckled and she ducked around the corner of the kitchen, her cheeks flaming red and her breathing a bit choppy. Lincoln thought she was gorgeous.

6

THE WITNESS

S upper was pleasant. That should be nice, but she was supposed to be showing Lincoln what a mess her life was; instead, her parents loved him. Her mother simpered all through dinner, practically feeding him herself. Her father chatted about horses, the weather, things that needed to be done in the barn as soon as he was able, and more inane rumblings. She should be happy. She hadn't seen her parents so animated in a long time. *Son of a b—*

Time to get out of the house. "Okay, well, I'll head out to the barn to start feeding the horses."

Her father's blue eyes landed on her. "Honey, Brian Lochlain came over this morning and took one of the gravity feeders to the grand bay field for me. If you could take the second one out to the mare's pasture, I'd appreciate it."

"What did he fill it with?"

"He cut the north hayfield this morning for us. He'll rake some each day to fill the wagons."

Locking eyes with her father, she waited for further

explanation but received none. As nice as Brian Lochlain was, why would he begin working on their farm for no money? And there wasn't much, that was certain. The medical bills had begun rolling in about nine months ago and without taking breeding jobs, there was precious little left over. Their savings accounts were all but depleted.

"Okay. I'll do that first."

Her father nodded. "Take the pickup."

The pickup, not the tractor. "Daddy, did you give him ...?"

Using his arms to push himself away from the table, he dismissed any further comment from her. "Lincoln, mind helping me get to the bathroom?"

Lincoln stood, and in four easy strides, he was around the table and at her father's side, helping him to stand and pulling his walker forward.

Her mother then shooed her away. "Go on, dear. Your work clothes are in your bedroom."

Quickly walking to the steps that took her upstairs to the four large bedrooms where she and her siblings slept, her mind raced. It was as if she had been transported to an alternate universe. Her father asked Lincoln for help. Her mother's face had a bit of a glow to it. And her father likely gave Brian Lochlain their tractor in exchange for field work. That was all well and good, but what would happen when they needed to plant next year? Soon, there would be nothing left to give away.

Pulling her black cami off, she tossed it on the bed, then quickly unzipped her skirt and stepped from it, laying it on the bed next to her cami. Glancing around the room but trying not to be nostalgic, she smiled at her track ribbons still tacked to the wall above her desk. Her mother still came up here once a week, dusted each room, and did her work laundry and kept it up here for her each day. They'd been fortunate growing up. They each had their own rooms, but they were all close. Just not physically. Her siblings were now spread out all over the nation. Except her brother, Devin, who was in River's Edge about forty-five miles away. But he ran his father-in-law's hardware store and between that, two boys in baseball and numerous other sports, he had little time for visiting. It was sad that they'd gotten too busy to be a family.

Descending the steps, she schooled her features to neutral. What could her father do? They had horses they needed to feed, and money was dwindling, if not already gone. But still, when Lincoln wasn't around, she'd find out what deal had been made and see what would need to be done for next year. Only her mother was in the kitchen, and as she entered from the stairwell, she noticed her mother's cheeks tinted pink. Shaking her head at the "Lincoln effect," she bit her lips to keep the smile from forming.

"Thank you, sweetheart, for bringing Lincoln over. I didn't know you were seeing anyone."

"I'm not. We aren't dating. I only met him today."

Her mother turned from the sink and the dishes soaking in the steaming water within, wiped her hands on the towel still tucked into the waistband of her jeans and locked eyes with hers. Her mother's brows rose into her bangs—bangs the same blonde as her own. They also shared the same blue Scandinavian eyes, though Skye was an inch or two taller.

"You just met him and yet you invited him to dinner? What do you know about him?"

"I think he's a cop or something. He's got the police dog in his truck. He came to work this morning and took one of our employees into custody. He's handsome and he's persistent. He asked me out, and I said I had things to do. He said he wanted to help." She shrugged her shoulders to convey the message that she was at a loss and watched her mother shake her head and turn back to her dishes, allowing her to take a breath. Deciding to take the dismissal as a sign she'd not have to argue any further, she strode across the kitchen to the mud room. Sitting on the bench alongside the wall, she quickly pulled on her barn boots and sucked in a deep breath. Releasing it as she stood, she listened for Lincoln and her father and could hear them walking down the hall to her parents' bedroom. Her father often napped after supper these days. Just getting to the table tired him out. But right now, he was listening as Lincoln told him a story about being in the service. She had to fight not to stay and listen.

Stepping quietly from the house, she walked across the yard to the barn as she pulled her long hair into a ponytail. There, she was able to let some of her tension fall away. They had two foals in stalls, each a beauty in its own right, dark chestnut in color, black manes, and large brown eyes. They offered so much pleasure she took the time to lean over the tops of each pen and admire their little faces and playful hopping around, nickering to each other. Noting that their pen needed to be mucked and fresh straw added before she could go home, she pushed away from the pens and walked to the back of the barn, opened the large door, and revealed the filled gravity wagon and her father's green pickup.

Only two attempts today to line the hitch with the tongue of the wagon. At least something was going right. Securing the wagon to the truck, she headed off the bumpy lane to the back pasture they called the mare's pasture. Back in the day, each of their pastures were named and those names stuck. As their herd dwindled, and they'd sold off one of the pastures, they continued to graze the few horses they had in different pastures to keep them fed and healthy but also to utilize the full ranch. They'd soon need to sell off another pasture depending on the deal her father had now made with Brian.

Admiring the fields and rolling hills of her family ranch, a bit of nostalgia settled heavy in her chest. While none of her siblings or she had wanted to run the ranch, she'd never dreamed they'd lose it. Where would her parents go if they had to sell it all?

Pulling to the gate of the mare's pasture, she looked around and saw three horses running toward her. Supper was served. She chuckled at their enthusiasm for fresh hay, quickly drove the pickup and hay wagon through the gate, and then unhooked the wagon as the horses munched happily on their supper.

She watched them for only a moment, knowing there was more work to finish before she could go home tonight. There she'd dig through her briefcase and research what was going on at Limitless. It didn't seem right that she shouldn't want their employees to be law-abiding citizens. Mangus' reaction was especially concerning. Of the two brothers, he was the most business minded and had stressed to her the importance of following their procedures.

Closing the gate, she hopped back into the truck and decided to take the lane around the grand bay pasture and see if there was any hay left in that wagon. From a distance she saw the glint of something in the pasture on the other side of the grand bay pasture and squinted her eyes to try and make out what it was. Going slowly so she didn't bounce around or wreck the truck, she kept her eyes on the object catching the sun's rays.

As she neared the gravity wagon along the fence line of the grand bay pasture, she realized the glint was a pickup truck. White in color but not one she recognized. Pulling to a stop just behind the gravity wagon, she hopped out of the truck and inched her way along the wagon to peer around and watch the truck on their property. Both doors opened on the white truck and two men stepped out, one on either side. They walked to the box of the truck and pulled the tailgate down. Reaching in, they pulled a man from the box, his arms tied behind his back, his face bloodied, and he seemed unable to stand or walk as they each grabbed an arm and dragged him a few feet from the truck.

Her heartbeat raced as she watched, not sure what she should do but feeling vulnerable being a witness to something like this. And who were these people? Then she saw one of the men, dark complexioned with a shaved head, pull a gun from the inside of his waistband and shoot the bloodied man in the head. The sound traveled to her ears as she covered her mouth with both hands. Her legs shook to the point she worried if she'd be able to make it back to the truck. They'd surely see her if she drove away now.

She watched, as the men jumped into their truck and drove away, until her vision blurred from the tears flooding her eyes. Dropping to her knees, she bowed her head and prayed for the dead man lying in her father's field and her family who would surely be brought into something they didn't want to be a part of. Allowing the tears to flow for only a moment or two longer, she slowly inhaled and swiped the tears on her cheeks. Swallowing to calm herself while rubbing her mascara-stained fingers on her jeans, she took a final deep breath and slowly stood, using a fence post as an anchor. Standing on shaky legs, she gave herself a moment more before making her way to her truck. After climbing in, she quickly locked the doors and sat stony-faced and numb, not sure what to do next. Patting her jeans' pockets, she realized her phone was still in her car. She'd been so rattled by Lincoln she'd forgotten the rule to never go to the pasture without your phone in case someone needs you or vice versa. She'd no doubt have to hear that lecture again.

"Okay, I can do this." She whispered. Telling herself to be strong helped a bit, but not much. She didn't want to drive past the body but she noted the clump of trees close to where the body of a man—she hoped like hell she didn't know—lay and slowly backed the pickup to the turnoff of the far path where she'd be able to turn around.

It felt as if it took an eternity to get back to the barn, and she was exhausted from watching every field and every lane to make sure the white pickup was nowhere to be seen, and more importantly, that they didn't see her.

Parking behind the barn, she heaved out a long breath and rotated her head. Her shoulders had tightened to the point that it was difficult doing just that much. Closing her eyes for a moment, she tried to mentally prepare herself for what was to come next—tell her parents and call the cops.

Entering the barn from the back, she was greeted with Lincoln's ass. The view was amazing, his muscular legs slightly bent as he worked to remove the soiled straw from the foals' pen. The T-shirt he wore was dampened in the middle of his back and just as her eyes traveled to his perfectly shaped, rounded ass, he turned, and she was greeted with his mighty fine, if not bulky ... um, front.

"Eyes up here, lady."

Her eyes snapped to his, and his smile instantly faded. "What happened to you?"

Her brows pressed together as she watched his eyes roam over her face. "Why were you crying?"

"How do you ...?" But the tears began to form again, and she cleared her throat, tossed her head in irritation, and responded. "I, um ... think I saw something. Bad. Something very bad."

He set the pitchfork along the stall wall, and stepped toward her. His knees bent slightly so he could see her at eye level, those smoky gray orbs took in her whole face.

"Tell me what you saw."

"I saw a man being killed." Her lips trembled and her knees threatened to buckle as if saying it out loud seemed to finally make it real. She reached out to hold on to him; he immediately recognized her predicament and swooped her up into his arms, carrying her to the bench at the far end of the barn.

7

—————

THIS IS BAD

Setting her on the bench, he kneeled in front of her, taking her shaking hands in his. Watching her lips tremble and feeling the shaking of her body had him more concerned than ever. She saw a man get killed?

"Princess, you need to tell me what you saw."

Her eyes bore into his, and despite the concern he felt, he had to admit they were the most perfect shade of blue he'd ever seen. Her mother's eyes, for certain. He tucked loose strands of her silky blonde hair behind her ear and let his fingers rest alongside her neck, adding just enough pressure that she'd feel his presence until her shaking subsided. After a few moments, she swallowed.

"I saw a white pickup out on the other side of the grand bay field. I was going to check on the hay in that wagon. I saw two men get out of the truck." She stifled a sob, and he ran his thumbs along her jaw in soothing motions, enjoying the feel of her warm skin against his. "They got out and pulled a bloodied man from the back, then one of the men shot the man. Then they left."

Her eyes sought his, and he willed his now racing heart to slow. "Is he dead?"

Her lips parted, but no sound was uttered. She raised her shoulders just a hair, closed her mouth, and then tears flowed down her soft cheeks. "I was afraid to go look." Swallowing, she inhaled deeply then continued. "They shot him in the head. I saw his head fly back before I even heard the sound." She began bouncing her knees and blinking furiously.

Sitting up on his knees, he pulled her head to his chest and held her close. Questions raced through his mind, but he wanted to give her a moment to calm down. He lay his cheek against the top of her head and inhaled her scent. She smelled of hay and oranges. Her hands grabbed hold of his T-shirt at his sides and his arms tightened around her.

"It'll be okay, princess."

"I'm not a princess."

He chuckled, inhaled once more, then reluctantly pulled away.

Holding her chin between his thumb and forefinger, he looked deeply into her eyes. "Did the two men see you?"

She shook her head but continued to stare at him. "You sure?"

"Yeah." It came out as a whisper.

"Can you identify them?"

"I don't ... I didn't recognize them. But, if I saw a picture I might be able to."

"Okay." He pulled his cell phone from his back pocket. "You should have called me or the police when you saw it so more time hadn't passed and maybe they'd be able to catch them."

"I ..." She looked away and toward their vehicles and the house and swallowed. "I forgot my phone. And, I don't have your number."

Turning her face to his, he took a deep breath, the chills of what could have happened finally settling into his gut. "Princess, you can't do that ever again. If they would have seen you, your phone may have been the only way we'd be able to find you. Do you understand?"

She nodded slightly, and he felt so bad for her. Normal people don't see this underbelly of society. Normal people never see someone killed. Normal people don't have to feel as though they aren't safe on their own property. But, princesses should never see that side of life. "When we get to the house, I'll make sure you have my number and I have yours."

Without waiting for a response he dialed 911, and they both stood at the same time. He took her hand in his and the size difference couldn't be overlooked. Her hand felt so small and delicate, and yet, perfect.

"9-1-1, what's your emergency?"

He walked them across the yard toward the house as he began relaying the information she'd given him. His hand was jerked as she abruptly stopped, and when he turned to see what was wrong, he saw her looking at the road toward the end of the driveway as a white pickup truck slowly passed by.

He tugged her to keep her moving and not call attention to themselves. They were sitting ducks out in the open if those men decided to shoot first and ask questions later. Noting quickly that the truck had a broken taillight and a deep scratch on the bottom of the driver's door, he led her quickly to the house. After entering, he locked the doors as he continued relaying information to the emergency operator.

Standing in the mud room, he pocketed his phone and turned to face Skye. Her face had paled, her hands trembled, and she looked lost.

His fingers floated across her cheek, then cupped her nape. "Was that the truck, Skye?"

Swallowing quickly, she nodded.

He took a deep breath. "Okay, we're going to go in there and tell your parents what's happening."

"No, I don't want them to know."

"Honey, the police will be here soon, and they need to know so they aren't blindsided."

"My dad ..."

"He'll be fine. He's stronger than you think."

His fingers squeezed her nape, and she nodded but said nothing. Turning, he placed his hand at her lower back and walked with her into the back of the house to her parents' bedroom. She knocked on the door and her mother instantly invited her in.

The surprise was apparent on both her parents' faces when they took in the sight of Lincoln standing next to her. He could still feel Skye's faint trembling and spoke first. "We need to talk."

Her parents looked at their daughter, then to him, then back to Skye. Jeff lay in bed, still clothed, but reclined as if he'd been napping. Her mother sat in a chair next to the bed in front of a window reading a book.

Jeff spoke first. "It'll take me a moment to get up."

"We can talk here. But you'll need to get up when the police get here."

"Police?" Melissa gasped, her eyes assessing her daughter closer.

Quickly retelling her story, Skye filled them in just before the squad car pulled into the driveway. Abe began barking and Lincoln excused himself to calm the dog down. Jeff spoke before he left the room. "You can bring him in, Linc. It'll be fine, and he can eat something."

"Thank you," he responded before hustling out to get his boy and speak to the cops.

Relief flooded through him when he saw his friends, Jerry Robards and Randy St. John, exiting the squad car. He simmered Abe down, opened the door, let him out, and watched as he ran to a tree on the property to do his business. Both officers laughed and approached him.

"You acted quickly, I see," Robards commented as they shook hands.

"It's not like that. I saw her alongside the road." He pointed behind him to her car with his thumb. "Her car overheated and I followed her home. Then things got weird."

He whistled to Abe and ushered the officers into the house to speak with Skye. After they entered the mud room, Lincoln led them into the kitchen where Skye was waiting for them. Her color hadn't come back yet, and she stood stock-still, her hands clasped tightly together in front of her. Glancing quickly at each officer, her eyes then sought his, and he moved closer to her before he introduced them to each other.

"Guys, why don't we all sit down?" He pointed to the kitchen table and chairs then turned to Skye. "Does your dad need help, hon?"

"Yeah. That'd be great. Mom's helping him now, but it seems so easy when you do it."

He pulled a chair away from the table and waited for her to sit. "I'll be right back, guys."

Quickly heading down the hall, he knocked on the bedroom door and was greeted with a terse, "Yeah?"

He cracked open the door and saw Jeff sitting at the side of the bed, head bent and breathing heavy. Melissa stood waiting next to him. "Wondered if you were interested in my help," Lincoln offered with a grin.

Jeff glanced at Melissa. "Go on in with our girl; I'll be right there."

She patted him on the shoulder and smiled as she passed him near the door.

"Okay, muscle man, come and help me up." Jeff's gruff mannerisms brought a chuckle from his belly, and he quickly stepped over to stand in front of him. Bending and grabbing his belt from behind, he waited briefly while Jeff grabbed his shoulders then hefted him up quickly. Once he was standing, Jeff huffed out a breath and steadied himself.

"How do you know how to do that?"

He ran his fingers along his nape, then responded honestly, "My friend, Mark, was injured in the service by an IED. His back was broken, and he had balance issues from the damage to his ears. I helped him every day during his recovery and learned a lot about lifting, standing, recovery—you name it."

Jeff's deep blue eyes, while not the same as Skye's light blue, were earnest and thoughtful. "You're a good friend. Not many would do that."

"He was a good friend to me."

"Was?"

"Yes sir." He tried not to let the sadness wash over him that usually did when he thought of Mark. Such a bright light now gone too soon always hurt his heart. "He ended his life a year after his accident."

Jeff nodded once, then took his walker in both hands and began to walk from the room.

Staying by his side, he walked the painfully slow pace making sure this man didn't fall or need assistance, but his gut wanted him in the kitchen with Skye. He knew she was freaking out while trying so hard to be strong, and he wanted to be there to support her. When they finally entered the kitchen, the small talk that had been going on halted as Melissa jumped up from her seat and pulled another chair to the table for her husband. She motioned with her hand to a chair next to Skye for him to sit, and Jeff slowly settled himself in the chair next to his wife.

Lincoln introduced the officers to Jeff, and Jerry began the questioning. Skye answered as clearly as she could and kept her composure until Randy St. John told her they'd need her to come with them to find the body. Wrapping his arm around her shoulders, he could feel her trembling, so he softly asked, "Would you mind if I came with you?"

She looked at him then and tried to smile, but it seemed forced. "Yes, please. I mean, no, I don't mind."

He nodded. "Shall we go now? I can take my truck if you guys want to follow us."

Both officers stood and agreed, and then shook Jeff and Melissa's hands before stepping to the door.

Glancing at Abe, who lay on a rug in front of the refrigerator, he told his pup to stay. He held Skye's hand as he walked her to his truck and helped her inside. He grabbed food for Abe from the back of his truck. He always carried food and water for Abe because sometimes they were out late. He tried to keep his feeding time regular.

Hustling the food back inside, he saw Abe's tail

wagging as Melissa began opening the bag and pouring the food into a dish. She would be his friend for life now.

Time to go find a dead body.

8

MIGHT AS WELL DIVE IN

~

She didn't get out of the truck—she couldn't. She'd never seen a dead body before, not one that wasn't already embalmed, made up, and in a casket anyway. Animals, sure. Growing up on a horse ranch, she saw all kinds of things. But not dead humans. She didn't want to see this man's face in her nightmares. Bad enough she'd see him being dragged and shot. That was gory enough for her.

She stared out the windshield of Lincoln's truck and watched as the officers took pictures, measured the perimeter around the body and where the shell casing landed. They measured tire tracks, casted them, examined the wounds on the man's body, and wrote things down. The forensic team that had come out had gotten to work immediately, and the proficiency with which they worked was a marvel. If it weren't so gruesome. She wondered for the hundredth time how they could do this for a living.

Lincoln continually looked in her direction to make

sure she was okay. He'd come to check on her about five or six times since they'd come out here. She had to admit to herself that he was wonderfully sweet and very solicitous toward her and her family. She'd never met a man who was so sweet and didn't want something in return. She guessed there was a first time for everything.

Watching him talk to the officers, they acted like old friends. A detective had arrived on scene about an hour ago and they'd chatted with each other for a long time. She grew uneasy when the detective finally glanced her way and then came to speak with her. But Lincoln was right there with her, holding her hand. The detective said his name was Rory.

"Ready to go back to the house?"

She jumped when Lincoln opened the door, she'd been so lost in her own head.

"Yes, please. My parents must be worried sick."

He started the truck and backed up, much faster than she ever could and spoke at the same time. "There's been an officer at the house with them all this time."

"Why?"

He stopped the truck and looked her in the eye. "Skye, you saw the white pickup driving past your parents' place. Now, they may or may not have seen you, but you can bet they know the cops are here and too fast for anyone to have found the body by accident."

"Oh my God." She swallowed. "Are they in danger? Am I in danger?"

"Don't know. But we're not taking any chances." She watched his jaw tighten, but those stony gray eyes stared straight ahead. That answered her question more than anything else did.

The drive back to the house was quiet, both of them

lost in their own thoughts. She just wanted to go home, take a long hot shower, and hide under the covers for a week. She hoped she'd sleep but that was doubtful because all she could see when she closed her eyes was that poor man being dragged from the back of the truck, his head flying back, and then the gunshot ringing in her ears.

Pulling his truck up next to her car once again, he let out a long breath before saying, "Princess, we're going to have to stay here tonight. We don't know what we're dealing with, and we need time to arrange security for you and your parents."

Did she just hear that right? Security. Her and her parents. She was beginning to go from scared to pissed. Now she'd be a prisoner in her parents' home.

"How long?"

He twisted in the seat and she marveled at how small the truck felt with him in it. Especially when it had felt so big and lonely while she'd sat in it by herself the past hour and a half.

"We don't know, hon. But we can have an officer relieve me around two in the morning, and then I can get some shuteye. You and your parents will be safe. Plus, we have Abe. He hears every little noise, so I'll apologize right away because you may not get much rest."

He grinned at her, and she couldn't help herself, she sighed. Now she sounded just like her mother.

She took a deep breath, released it, then nodded before she opened the door and jumped down from the truck. Circling around the front of it, she went to her car, pulled her phone and briefcase from the front seat and began walking to the house, Lincoln at her side.

***

Three hours later, her parents finally tucked in for the night, she pulled her laptop from her briefcase along with the files she'd taken from work and set them up on the kitchen table. Lincoln was in the living room, securing windows and settling Abe for the night. Her mom had spoiled Abe silly already by making a bed for him in front of the sofa with two quilts so it would be soft. Lincoln just shook his head as he watched her fuss and told her he didn't need all of that bedding, but she ignored him.

It took Abe three minutes to hop on the soft bed, scratch around and mess it all up, then settle himself in nicely. Her mom, pleased with herself and Abe, smiled, looked Skye in the eye, and winked as she left the kitchen and walked to her bedroom. She had already made up the bed in Skye's brother Logan's room for Lincoln. Subtle was not her mother. And, she still sighed a little when she was in close proximity of Lincoln. Honestly, she didn't know how she'd ever get him out of her life once this was all over. Her parents—both of them—would hate her.

Reading over the file on Steven Vann, she saw immediately that no background check had been run on him. Deciding she'd run one herself, she typed his name in the usual databases and pulled up a very long list of crimes the man had committed. Burglary, armed robbery, assault with a deadly weapon, domestic disputes, drug charges. The man had no redeeming qualities at all. She'd never have hired him, so why had Victor?

Pulling up the files on the other two employees Victor had hired without her knowledge, Marco Rodriguez and Giuseppe Russo were of a similar ilk.

Lincoln entered the kitchen and stared at her for a moment, then took the seat next to her at the table. "What's keeping you up so late?"

Rotating her head, she reached back and massaged her neck to ease the tension coiling in her muscles only to have Lincoln softly remove her hands and take up in her place. "Relax your shoulders, princess."

He pressed deep into the tight balls in her shoulders. "Take a deep breath." She did as she was told and he held his thumbs on the tightness, which sort of hurt. "Now, breathe out." She exhaled and found she was able to relax just a bit. "One more time."

By the third time, she was able to let some of the tension go. He kneaded her muscles a bit more, then asked her again, "What are you working on, princess?"

She giggled just a bit. "I'm not a princess. I don't know why you keep calling me that."

"Honest to God, Skye, the first time I saw you, I thought you looked like a fairy princess. Blonde flowing hair, impeccable posture, graceful fluid movements. When you speak, you're refined and elegant. A princess."

She stared at him. His face, his eyes never wavered, and she was unable to look away. He thought something of her she'd never felt. She always wanted to be like a princess, all graceful and beautiful. But she was a farm girl, usually covered in shit or dirt, wearing grubby jeans and T-shirts, and always smelled like hay, poop, or horse. She'd never met anyone who thought she looked like a princess. Ever.

He leaned toward her, slowly, and her stomach flipped at the realization that he was going to kiss her. She'd be lying if she said she hadn't thought of it during the day. Especially after she'd first met him. During dinner she couldn't stop watching his mouth—his lips—as he spoke, ate, smiled. And that lock of hair that rested against his forehead. Damn, her fingers itched to touch it.

Thoughts ran rampant at that moment. Her breath was likely bad. Her hair still looked like hell; the ponytail now sat askew and to the side tilting at a weird angle. Her makeup had been smudged and rubbed from her crying, so no doubt she looked more like an evil witch than any princess. And Lincoln still wanted to kiss her.

Their lips touched and the shiver ran the length of her body and settled in her most private of places. Dampness grew and her nipples puckered. Damn, he was a great kisser.

His soft lips molded to hers, moving in the most delicious way, and she lost all thought and opened her mouth, allowing his tongue to slide in. She whimpered at the feel, so wet and supple, and the way his tongue moved sent gooseflesh rippling over her entire body.

He tilted his head and their mouths fused together like they were meant to be. A soft moan escaped from somewhere deep inside her, and the feeling of falling engulfed her. Quickly pulling back, she blinked and fought for control of her emotions. And, where was her brain right now? All thought had left her except how Lincoln felt. She couldn't let that happen again. She didn't have time for a man in her life—or what she called a life.

"Uh." She took in a deep breath and tried again. "I should get back to work." Her voice was soft, and her excuse sounded weak and unconvincing, but she couldn't let herself fall.

"Okay, so tell me what you're working on, and maybe I can help."

"It's just stuff I didn't finish at work." She still wasn't sure how much she should share with him.

"Confidential stuff?"

Huffing out a breath, she glanced at her computer

screen, but not before he did. His brows shot up into his dark shiny hair and her thoughts jumbled over themselves imagining him as Prince Charming with his classic good looks, massive size, and good-natured manner. As a matter of fact, he was damned near perfect.

He read the reports then pulled Steven Vann's up to read further. His eyes bounced back and forth between the documents on the table and her computer screen. But, he'd have known all of this anyway since they first met because he brought Vann into custody. Watching him compare all three reports, she tried not to be offended that he seemed lost in the reports and she was all but forgotten.

Probably for the better anyway. She picked up each report as he set them down, and soon realized what had captured his attention. Each of the men had ties to the pawn shop in town. Not just ties, but had been arrested at one time or another in the pawn shop. Selling stolen goods and Giuseppe Russo for selling drugs. What was even weirder was they'd each gotten out of jail every time for these arrests and their attorney was none other than Limitless International's Corporate Counsel, Walter Goldman.

"Why would you hire these guys?"

"I didn't. That's the problem."

He turned in his chair to face her. "Then who did?"

The feeling of defeat fell heavy on her chest. Maybe it was dread. "Victor Santarino hired them."

The constant tension of the day and sitting hunched over her computer for these past few hours tightened her muscles. Sitting back, she stretched as much as she could in her chair. Pulling the band from her ponytail, she rubbed her scalp to ease the soreness where it tugged at her head. "I just don't understand why."

"So, you had nothing to do with bringing these men into the corporation?" He was studying her so intently, the muscles in the back of her neck tightened up and the pounding headache that was beginning to grow forced her to stand suddenly, almost toppling her chair.

"No. And for the record, I got my ass reamed today for handing Steven Vann over to you. That's why I wanted to check these guys out myself. I have no idea what's going on there."

Packing up her files and closing the lid on her laptop, she tucked everything into her briefcase. She'd take some aspirin for her headache and try to get some sleep. Maybe tomorrow everything would be brighter. How did the song go? "Tomorrow, tomorrow, there's always tomorrow" or something.

He muttered, "We wondered why you handed him over."

9

NOT GOING THERE AGAIN

The look on her face said volumes. He hadn't meant for her to hear him, and now, her back was ramrod straight, and her usually soft supple lips were pressed into a fine line. Fuck.

"What does that mean? And who is 'we'?" She said it so slowly, he felt the hairs on the back of his neck stand. Her voice didn't even sound like hers.

Inhaling deeply, he stood and took the two steps to get into her space. The question here was, how honest could he be? Best to start with the easier part of that question. "'We' means the Lynyrd Station PD."

Standing this close, he could still smell a hint of the fresh citrusy perfume she wore. How could it be she'd still smell delicious after the day she'd had? Probably because she wore expensive perfume. Just like her expensive shoes and clothes.

"Why are the police speculating on why I'd turn over someone who'd broken the law?"

His eyes raked over her long hair, the fine lines at the corners of her eyes, and the dark circles that had formed over the last couple of hours. His fingers tingled with want of touching her. He needed to rein that shit in. He'd promised himself when he moved to Lynyrd Station that he'd never get involved again with a high-maintenance, drama-filled woman. His ex-wife did him in with that bullshit.

"Not you necessarily, just Limitless."

"Why Limitless?"

Rubbing the back of his neck with one hand to lay the tiny hairs down, while stuffing the other in his front pocket to keep from touching Skye, he let out a long breath. "There are things going on there that the cops are watching. And, for the record, I'd appreciate it if you kept that to yourself for a while."

"Things? What things?"

"Skye, hon, I can't share that with you. But, you need to be careful. And, while we're on the subject, who reamed your ass for turning Vann over?"

There wasn't a lot of space between them, but enough for her to put shields up in the form of arms crossed over her lovely breasts. "I asked you a question first."

"And I answered that I can't divulge that information." To keep from crossing his arms, he shoved his free hand into his other front pocket and schooled his features into a neutral expression.

She rotated her head and he felt bad. She'd been through a grueling day and there were likely many more to come before this was all over with.

"Go to bed, princess. Get some rest and we'll continue our discussion tomorrow."

A look of defeat washed over her gorgeous face, and he couldn't stop himself from pulling her into his arms. Son of a bitch, she felt good pressed against him. Soft in all the right places and she let out a little sigh. All he could do was close his eyes and lay his cheek against the top of her head.

His thumb rotated tiny circles on her back and his heartbeat kicked up. Swallowing the giant lump in his throat, he managed to speak softly. "Go to bed, princess."

Tightly squeezing her to him, he released her, and stepped back.

Her face tilted up to his, and he noticed instantly that she'd lost the anger she'd had only moments before. Without another word, she took a step back, grabbed her briefcase, and proceeded to the stairs disappearing one step at a time. He listened to her footsteps move across the floor above him and imagined her getting undressed for bed. That thought sent his body into overdrive in certain places and he forcibly had to think of anything else. Dead bodies were a good place to start. Criminals and dead bodies. That should get him through the night.

Letting out a long slow breath, he turned out the kitchen lights and peered out the windows, looking for anything suspicious. Satisfied all was well, he slowly walked into the living room and sat on the sofa. Abe stood, stretched, and dutifully sat at his feet, chin resting on his knee. He softly petted Abe's forehead and down his neck offering a good scratch where his collar rested. "I'm getting myself in trouble here, boy."

Abe's tail thumped.

*

Two hours later and all he could think of was Skye in bed—maybe naked—above him while he sat down here with his dog. After his divorce, he'd vowed to keep his head where women were concerned. After his ex had bled him dry, all because of her expensive taste, he'd finally woken up to the fact that he was nothing more than a wallet to her. He wanted kids. He'd overlooked so much to have a family—little ones on his knee, the dog, the house, and a white picket fence. Well, maybe not the fence, but the good ole American dream. It didn't happen, and as he thought on it now, it was probably for the best. Wrong woman, wrong time, wrong everything.

Lights sprayed across the window and the sound of a car pulling into the driveway reached his ears. Abe perked up and let out a bark.

"*Ruhig*!" he snapped, wanting to keep Abe as quiet as he could even though it wasn't in his nature. Peering out the window, he saw a Lynyrd Station patrol car and knew his relief had arrived. The bone tired weariness he'd been ignoring rushed at him full force. Pulling his fatigued body from the sofa, he clicked his tongue, commanding Abe to follow him through the kitchen and out the backdoor.

Randy St. John exited his squad car and met him on the steps.

Randy extended his hand. "Everything looks quiet here."

"It has been so far; I hope it stays that way for all of our sakes."

"Agreed. You staying or going?" His grin said volumes though Lincoln ignored it.

"Staying. Melissa set up a bedroom for Abe and me upstairs. If anything happens, I'm your backup."

St. John chuckled. "Sounds like a plan. Go to bed, I've got this."

Only too eager to comply, Lincoln hustled Abe into the house and trudged up the stairs carrying Abe's makeshift bed. Though he usually let Abe sleep at the foot of the bed with him, it was his one concession where Abe was concerned. During training the instructors stressed the boundary between alphas and betas, but he wanted Abe to rest comfortably so he'd be rested for anything they had going during the day. It didn't make them equals to get a good night's sleep, and Abe never tested the relationship.

Unable to resist, he stopped at the closed door on the left at the top of the stairs where Skye slept now. Listening intently, he couldn't hear her breathing. Abe whimpered softly, and he knew his pup was tired. He turned to the open door directly across from Skye's and hustled his pup inside, softly closing the door behind him.

10

NOW WHERE DID HE GO?

~

She wanted to be gone before Lincoln came downstairs, and she needed to go home, take a shower, and dress for work. She'd snuck from her bedroom and into the kitchen without a sound. Her mother was already up making breakfast. Pouring a fresh cup of coffee into a travel mug, one of the plethora of mugs her mom seemed to horde, she topped it off with a dash of creamer, kissed her mom on the cheek then her dad, and quickly made her way out the door. Feeling relieved, she stopped short when Lincoln stood next to her car, tossing the ball for Abe to fetch.

Inhaling deeply, she continued to her car, tossed her briefcase onto the passenger seat and turned to face him. Dammit. He'd had all of four hours of sleep and yet he looked ... impeccable. His lips formed the perfect smile, and she stopped herself from sighing. Geez that was annoying. She wasn't a young and stupid schoolgirl for crying out loud. She seriously needed to get over this crazy flutter in her tummy and the little sighs as he did absolutely nothing but look at her.

"I thought you were still sleeping."

"Ah, so you thought you'd sneak out of the house while I was sleeping? Who would protect you?"

"I don't need ..." She stopped when she saw his brows rise into the lock of hair that fell over his forehead. That shiny, perfect dark lock. She found herself staring at it. That was until he responded.

"Princess, maybe while you're at work you're safe. But we still don't know who killed the man in the field. We don't know who the man was. We don't know if they saw you last night. As a matter of fact, we don't know anything at this point."

Huffing out a breath, she allowed herself to get lost in those stormy gray eyes for a brief moment, then she decided to get mad.

"I'm to be a prisoner then? Watched constantly as if I've done something wrong?"

Picking up and tossing the ball Abe dropped at his feet, he turned to her once again. "Not a prisoner. But we don't know who's out there and if they mean you harm. So, you'll need to be escorted to and from work and any other place you want to go. With your car not especially reliable, we can't have you stopped alongside the road, vulnerable for anyone to do you harm."

A Lynyrd Station PD squad pulled into the driveway. A female officer stepped from her vehicle.

Shaking hands with Lincoln, it wasn't lost on Skye that the female officer blushed as she touched his hand and was reluctant to let the handshake end. Turning to her, the officer said, "I'm here to escort you to the office, Ms. Sommers. My name is Kara Dean." Kara held out her hand, and Skye shook it firmly. Maybe a bit stronger than was needed. Kara's eyes squinted as she stared back at her.

Feeling a little sheepish at her behavior, she feigned a smile. "You're just in time, I'm ready to leave now. I'll be stopping at my apartment for a shower and a change of clothing first, then going to the office."

Officer Dean nodded then turned to get into the squad car. Skye heard Lincoln chuckle and tossed her head while refusing to look at him.

Driving to her apartment, her mind raced with all manner of thoughts. She'd tossed and turned all night, held her breath when she heard Lincoln stop at her door, not sure if she wanted him to come into her room or not. After that, her thoughts bounced among Lincoln; her dad; her mom; Lincoln; Limitless; Lincoln; and criminals. Was she in trouble? And back to Lincoln.

He wasn't what she needed right now. Her ex-husband wasn't the man she'd thought he was. While he enjoyed the finer things in life, what she'd quickly realized after they married was he liked the good life, but he was lazy and wanted her to provide it for him. She'd worked two jobs the whole three years they were married. He was impossibly handsome, and the women in his life—his mother, sisters, and his female "friends"—had doted on him endlessly. She wasn't going down that road again, especially since her parents needed so much attention.

Checking her rearview mirror often, seeing Officer Dean following closely, her nose wrinkled. She hadn't made the best first impression. And, she certainly needed to get over her silly jealousy where Lincoln was concerned. She'd been turned by a pretty head before. Never again.

Pulling into the parking lot of her apartment complex,

she waited for Officer Dean to step out of her squad car before opening her door. Reminding herself to be nicer, she smiled before saying, "I won't be long. Please come inside and have a cup of coffee."

Seeing the surprise on the officer's face, she smiled again.

"Thank you, Ms. Sommers."

Entering her apartment, gooseflesh rose on her arms. How could it feel so darned good to be home after only one night away? Pouring fresh water into her instant coffee maker, she pointed to a basket of coffees for Officer Dean to choose from and began pulling out a cup, creamer, and sugar. "Help yourself. I'll only be a few minutes."

She then proceeded to her bedroom to gather her clothing and take a shower.

*

Feeling refreshed and ready to face the day, her heart skipped a beat as she pulled into the parking lot at Limitless, only to see Lincoln walking into the building. She'd specifically asked him not to come here again. Mangus had warned her in no uncertain terms that she wasn't to help him anymore. Of course, all of that was before she'd witnessed a murder and put her life and those of her parents in danger. She honestly had bigger things to worry about, but still, the fact that he purposely ignored her request rankled.

Well, he could just wait then, the stubborn, pigheaded Neanderthal with the sexiest eyes she'd ever seen. She glanced in her rearview mirror. Officer Dean had parked at the back of the lot with the nose of her squad car pointing to the building, scanning the area. Skye let out a deep breath. At least she wouldn't have to explain her presence in the building.

Walking to the loading docks, she entered through the dock door and into the shipping and receiving department. She'd just skirt the front of the building so Lincoln wouldn't see her. The men working there stopped and stared and the tiny hairs at the back of her neck prickled. The first person she recognized was Steven Vann. How the hell he'd gotten out of jail already was certainly a mystery, especially when she'd looked at his rap sheet.

Quickening her steps, she found the staircase leading up to the main offices. The dark stares from the men watching her sent chills running down her back, especially as one of the men pulled a large carpet from the trailer of a truck déjà vu of the men pulling that poor man from the pickup truck flooded her thoughts once again. Those men looked just ... Like. These. Men.

Jogging up the final few steps, she skirted the main area of the building and made her way to her office, gratefully avoiding everyone.

Closing her office door behind her, she leaned against it, her breathing heavy and choppy and her heart racing wildly. Did those men work here? Were they the ones? Had they seen her? Oh my God, she was in trouble. So. Much. Trouble.

Now, she hoped Lincoln would come to her office. Where was he anyway? Finally feeling as though her shaking knees would support her walk to her desk, she sat and turned her computer on. Closing her eyes as she waited for it to boot up, she practiced a deep breathing exercise—in and slowly out. In ... count to five ... slowly out. Her fingers stopped shaking and her heartbeat slowed enough to allow her to think.

When Lincoln came up here, she'd tell him what she saw, and he'd know what to do. She no longer felt safe here at Limitless, but she wasn't sure how she could leave. A knock on her door caused her to jump then freeze. The knock sounded again. Shaking her head and clearing her throat, she managed a weak, "Come in."

Sloane, Victor's assistant, entered wearing a bright smile on her face and holding a cup of coffee in each hand. "I brought you some coffee, so I could gossip a bit."

"Gossip? Well, is it good gossip or bad?" Her voice sounded normal—to her own ears, at least.

"Oh, so good. That hot cop who was in yesterday came back and asked Jeannine out to lunch."

Her stomach dropped to her feet, and the swallow of coffee she'd just taken suddenly tasted like a sour lemon. Setting her cup gently on her desk, she held her hands together in her lap and tried not to sound affected. "Do tell." Short and sweet. It was all she could manage at this point. She knew it. Handsome men couldn't be trusted. And Jeannine? Their receptionist? Oh, for crying out loud.

"Well, I guess they're going to have an early lunch today because she has to cover for me while I go to lunch, but, ooh-wee, lucky Jeannine."

"Right. Lucky Jeannine," she absently repeated.

Quickly standing, Sloane happily chirped, "Gotta run. Victor seems especially ornery today, so keep your head down."

11

THIS IS HOW YOU GATHER INFORMATION

Making his way up the steps of Limitless, Lincoln was both a bit concerned about how this might look to Skye and eager to do a good job. Ford had confirmed with Rory's contact that they were a go. Now he needed to get to work. He needed a bit more information, such as when shipments came in, where they were unloaded, what happened after that, and anything else he could find. He had a good idea that many of the key players were right here in this building, if not in Lynyrd Station. Helping Lynyrd Station PD arrest them and clean up this town were the highlight of his job. Both of his jobs.

Stepping through the thick glass doors, the soft music and fresh floral aroma washed over him. It was as if the world stopped the moment he stepped into this building and the hustle and bustle of the outside world vanished. That was probably the mental game for this company. Get buyers to slow down and never want to leave here. And, when they did leave, they'd do it with their pockets much lighter. At least the legitimate part of this business was about that.

Jeannine, the receptionist he'd met yesterday, sat behind her high-topped desk, her light brown hair pulled back in a ball at the back of her head. It looked painfully tight actually, and it did nothing for her appearance. Her ears looked unusually large with her severely styled hair, and the large, red-dangling hoops she wore accented the size of her ears. Her bright red lipstick looked like a sticky mess, and when she saw him and smiled, he noticed some of the lipstick smeared on her teeth. Good Lord, why did women wear that crap?

"Hi. Lincoln ... right?"

"Right. Jeannine ... correct?" He feigned interest because he needed this plan to work.

"Fabulous! You remembered. Yes, that's me." She giggled and tilted her head in what he supposed was a coy pose, but it made his neck hurt the way she froze in that position. "How can I help you today?"

Leaning on the top of the counter, he leaned in, shot her a drop-dead smile—at least, that's what he hoped it was—and stared into her eyes. "I was wondering if you'd like to have lunch with me."

She stammered and sputtered, and finally with a big lipstick-smeared, toothy smile replied, "Oh my God, yes, that would be lovely."

"Great, see you at noon at the Copper Cup for lunch? They have the best spareribs around."

"That sounds just perfect. Oh, except, can we do eleven o'clock instead? I have to fill in during lunch for Sloane, Victor's assistant."

Making a mental note that Sloane may have been a

better choice for information, he nodded, stepped back, and said, "I'll see you there at eleven."

Striding to the glass doors, a couple of things hit him at once. Skye's car was in the parking lot, but it hadn't been there earlier when he came in. He hadn't seen her come into the building either and there wasn't a cop car outside, so she'd been here for a little while.

First order of business this morning was to head up the mountain and fill in Ford and Dodge on the activities of last night and his plans for the day. He needed to make arrangements for Skye and her parents' safety. They wouldn't get the Lynyrd Station PD to offer round-the-clock protection for long. They needed to identify their dead body, find the killers, find out if any evidence pointed toward Skye as a witness, and the identity of the owner of the white pickup. Finally, the PD was rounding up photos to see if Skye could ID either of the men who'd shot the man in the Sommers' field.

A full day.

*

Seated at a booth toward the back of the Copper Cup and trying to look casual, he sent an email to Rory telling him the fed contact had checked out per Ford, and they have verified payment and details. Continuing to browse his phone for emails on what Ford had found for him by way of security, he found nothing of note yet. He hated waiting. He texted Dodge, who was at Sommers' Dream, to make sure no activity had taken place, and then he heard the clicking of high heels heading straight for him. Standing while placing his phone in his shirt pocket, he smiled as his eyes landed on Jeannine. He silently sent up a prayer that she'd wiped the lipstick from her teeth, so he could concentrate on getting information. He didn't want to have to do this again.

"Hi, Lincoln. I hope I haven't kept you waiting." Her clean smile relieved him a bit and he was able to relax his shoulders.

"Not at all. I only got here a few minutes ago." He held his hand toward the seat opposite him and waited as she scooted into the booth before sitting. He glanced at the waitress and waved, pleased that she hustled right over to take their order.

"I was so surprised that you asked me out today. Skye is some tough competition, and after meeting her yesterday, I figured you wouldn't have eyes for anyone else."

He didn't need to hear Skye's name right now. For the strangest of reasons, he had a heavy guilty heart just having lunch with Jeannine. Though there was no reason for it. He'd only just met Skye. One kiss. That was it. Plus, he wasn't interested in a high-maintenance woman loaded down with drama and issues. Nope. Didn't need that.

"You shouldn't sell yourself so short, Jeannine. Limitless seems like an interesting place to work. How long have you been there?"

She giggled from the compliment and he fought the urge to grind his jaws together. Funny, when Skye giggles he doesn't mind it at all. In fact, it's cute. "It is, and I started right when they opened. I was the first-floor employee that Mangus hired."

The waitress brought their iced teas and he took a moment to take a drink and run through his thoughts.

"Mangus and not Skye?"

"She'd just been hired and was learning about the company. She sat in on my interviews, and I suppose, practiced on me when it came to what the company wanted in terms of hiring and the process. Plus, I think Mangus has a little crush on Skye and likes to keep her close."

Right. He recalled the picture of Mangus and Skye at an event and how they stood close together. "I suppose it's hard not to grow close to a beautiful woman when you see each other every day."

"Hmm. I suppose." She took a drink of her tea, then sniped, "I'm sure his wife wouldn't think it was so great."

Well, that's interesting. "Mangus is married?"

"Yes, though I understand his wife lives in Italy and stays there most of the time. I guess she doesn't like America."

"That's hard on a marriage." He wondered about this bit of news and just how close Mangus and Skye were.

"Yep, I think it is. But, I suppose many of their activities are hard on a marriage. They both travel all over the world, Victor and Mangus. Victor mostly and always coming back with exotic jewelry, paintings, and oriental rugs for us to sell in the galleries. Though it does seem weird that he gets a lot of shipments, and by that, I mean a lot more than it seems we sell here in Lynyrd Station. I suppose we transfer it to some of the other locations for selling too. But every Tuesday and Wednesday our parking lot is full to the point that if I'm not in by 7:45 a.m., I'll have to park on the street out front."

Well, now we're getting somewhere. The waitress brought their ribs and his stomach growled as the tangy aroma wafted up to his nose. Jeannine giggled, and he caught her hungry look. One that didn't seem as though it included food. It was almost enough to sour his stomach, but not quite.

"Lynyrd Station is a rather small town; it must have been hard to find enough people to fill up that parking lot. How many employees does Limitless have?"

"Oh, Sloane just told me we now have fifty-eight employees. Though we only have a few of us that work the floor. The entire office staff includes two full-time accountants. Skye, of course, in HR. Victor and Mangus each have personal assistants. We have an inside sales department that has around ten employees, a couple gals in payroll, and the rest work in the shipping and receiving department. They almost outnumber us now."

"Are those shipping and receiving employees part-time? It seems that they don't come in every day."

"No. One of the girls in the payroll department complained that they're all paid full-time even though they're hardly here, and Victor has them doing other things for him when shipments are coming and going." She set her rib on her plate, wiped sauce from her fingers, then took a drink of tea. He watched her and felt bad for using her for information. But, he had a job to do, and he wondered if she'd get in trouble if anyone else at the office found out she had lunch with him. Victor and Mangus had laid into Skye pretty badly yesterday. "Of course, a few of the guys are always at Butch Ariens' place, loading and unloading items, so he's part of the group somehow."

"Butch Ariens, as in the owner of Black Gold Pawn?"

"One and the same."

"Strange. It doesn't seem as though a pawn shop and a place like Limitless would have anything to do with each other. Opposite ends of the spectrum."

"I know. Well, I hate to cut this short, but I have to get back and relieve Sloane. It sure was nice having lunch with you, Lincoln. Will I see you again?"

He stood as she did and responded. "Sure, I've got a busy rest of my week, but how about I stop by Limitless next week and set a date?"

"That sounds perfect. Gotta run."

He could hear her giggling as she walked out of the Copper Cup, and that's all he noticed. Lost in thought, he sat to finish his ribs and ponder all he'd learned. At least the lunch was fruitful in information. Now he just hoped Skye didn't find out about it.

12

BLACK GOLD PAWN

Lincoln sat in his truck outside Black Gold Pawn gathering his thoughts. He'd been here for more than an hour and hadn't once seen any of the key players in his file. Ford had done a great job of pulling information together on some of these guys. Basically, Limitless was a front for the Santarino family's illegal deals. Police suspected arms. Maybe drugs. They knew about the art and jewels, they just didn't know how they were stealing them and they needed air tight evidence to wrap up their case.

The fear was that the dead man in the Sommers' field had been an undercover agent, Jake Masters, who mostly worked out of the California arm of Limitless. They knew he'd come to town yesterday morning, had a meeting with Victor at Limitless, left to meet Butch Ariens, and never returned. They may get lucky and find that he was just with a whore and having a good time; But, Lynyrd Station PD was emailing pictures of the dead man and receiving pictures of Agent Masters, who worked for a special ops group called GHOST. Ford was trying to find out more about GHOST now.

Which brought him right back around to Butch. Apparently, Butch liked to gamble and owed the Santarino family big bucks. The suspicion is they were making him work off his debt by laundering supplies, arms, and money through the pawn shop.

Which brings us to now. For the first time since he'd left Arkansas, he was sorry he'd gotten into this mess. Bringing in guys who failed to show up for court was one thing. That had been the agreement when he, Ford, and Dodge had decided to open the agency, Big Three Bounty Hunters. But now, he was essentially going undercover, sort of, which was always dangerous, and infiltrating a crime family who was growing in strength. And now, murder was on the table.

Heaving out a big breath, he turned to Abe and commanded, "*Bleibe*," which meant stay. Patting Abe on the head and getting a lick on the cheek in return, he exited his truck, hitting the lock button on the fob as he walked toward Black Gold Pawn. A glance at his vehicle confirmed Abe was watching him intently, and that's how he'd stay until he returned. Abe's loyalty was impressive.

Schooling his features to neutral, he opened the door allowing one last deep intake and exhale of air. His heartbeat kicked up a few notches and he recalled why he'd left detective work. A dark-haired man stood behind the counter of the shop looking at his phone. He barely glanced up as Lincoln approached the counter.

"I'd like to see Butch."

That got his attention. Slowly looking up, the clerk—a good eight inches shorter than Lincoln—finally met his gaze. He lowered his phone, squinted his eyes, and stared without a sound. Lincoln gave him a little leeway, before leaning in slowly and lowering his voice. "I need an AK for my boss, and I was told by Victor Santarino to ask for Butch."

Without so much as a grunt, the clerk turned on his heel and walked to a back room. Lincoln stood at the counter for a few minutes but, as time passed, he began to look around the store, careful to continue facing the door the clerk had walked through. No need in getting stabbed in the back or accosted from behind when you could help it.

The front door opened and a younger man carrying three pizza boxes came into the building, walked directly behind the counter and through the door the clerk had just disappeared through.

A mental check for his weapons helped to put him at ease a bit. Ankle, kidney, and front pocket. Working to keep his face relaxed, he noted a few things about the place. The clerk knew the name Victor Santorino. The pizza delivery was likely a scam as the aroma of fresh hot pizza was nonexistent. The items for sale in the pawn shop all carried a heavy layer of dust showing no one moved or looked at these items in a very long time. This would also mean no sales, which meant they were keeping the doors open with money from another source.

Looking as casual as he could, he made his way to the front door where he inspected a camping setup on display of sorts. Questions ran through his mind, not the least of which, what was taking so fucking long? What was in the pizza boxes and how could Skye be involved in any of this?

The backdoor opened and the surly clerk stepped up

to the counter. "Butch is busy, and we don't have any AKs in the store."

He nodded his head. "Thanks." He stepped out the door and mid-inhale Skye's car was headed right toward him. The car was in the beginning stages of overheating again, and he both ground his teeth together and wondered why the hell she was driving around with her car like that, this late at night, and in front of Black Gold Pawn, no less.

She pulled to a stop as he stepped into the road, nearly in front of her car. As she rolled her window down, he barked, "What are you mixed up in, Skye?"

"I was just about to ask you the same thing."

The instant knot in his stomach sent a warning signal to his brain. "We can't talk here."

He stepped back toward his truck. "Follow me."

Hopping into his pickup, he began to pull away just in front of Skye and a sleek black Mercedes pulled into the driveway that lead to the back of the pawn shop. Making a mental note of the plate, which was California issue, he kept going, watching in his rearview mirror to make sure Skye was following him. The Mercedes stopped midway, and the chill that ran the length of his spine told him it was Victor and he'd seen Skye and him at Black Gold. Fuck. He'd bet his left nut that clerk had called him in and that had been the delay.

Double fuck.

13

FESSING UP

Holding her breath till her lungs burned and letting it out slowly kept her mind off the million things on it at this point. First of all, her day at work sucked. As in S.U.C.K.E.D. Sucked. Her tummy was in knots over Lincoln having lunch with Jeannine. Why would he do that? Then, not once, but twice, she'd seen Jeannine in the break room only to have to hear her tittering on about her lunch and how handsome Lincoln was and blah, blah, blah. The jealousy that had settled in the pit of her stomach was almost too much to bear. And why in the hell should she be jealous? Because he'd kissed her? That hardly meant anything. But, at least he hadn't kissed Jeannine. Sadly, she'd gotten a fair amount of satisfaction from that fact when Sloane had asked outright if he'd kissed her and Jeannine's face fell into a deep frown. "No, he was the perfect gentleman," was her comment. Which every woman knew meant he hadn't so much as tried to make a move. So, there was that.

Then, mysteriously Sloane had to go and retrieve Jeannine for some impromptu meeting with Victor. When

Jeannine left Victor's office, she was in tears and ran straight to the bathroom. She knew the feeling. That's how she'd felt yesterday when he'd chewed her out. She didn't want to seem nosy, so she refrained from asking questions, but the little bit she'd gotten from Sloane was that Victor found out about Jeannine's lunch date and he wasn't happy.

So, it was more apparent than ever that Victor didn't like Lincoln and wasn't afraid to let his employees know about this.

She'd managed to skirt him for the remainder of the day, mostly because he'd stomped down to the shipping and receiving area and spent the rest of the time she was at the office down there. Slipping out at exactly five o'clock on the dot, she drove home with a Lynyrd Station PD squad behind her to check on her parents only to find and meet Dodge Sager, Lincoln's friend and business partner, who was no slouch on the hot meter, so all wasn't lost. But, he'd told her he was on security detail until they figured out what they were all in for. She did chores, but was afraid to take hay out to the field and their neighbor, Brian Lochlain, had gone to do it at her father's request. As relieved as she was about not having to do it herself, she still worried about the state of affairs at home and what deal her father had made with Brian for all of his help.

Overhearing Dodge on the phone with Lincoln and learning that Lincoln was going to Black Gold Pawn, she knew she had to tell him about the events of the day and that he shouldn't go Limitless ever again since it sent Victor into a tizzy. She might have the courage to ask about Jeannine, but well, that was far from her mind right now. Right. That's why she was still trying to figure out how to bring it up. Sheesh.

Now, she was following Lincoln out of town, and in the corner of her eye she saw Victor's Mercedes pulling into the driveway of Black Gold Pawn. That couldn't have been coincidence. Had he seen her car? He'd probably heard it because it was beginning to run rough again, and honest to God, if Lincoln didn't turn off onto a side road soon, she'd be the sitting duck he'd warned her about this morning.

Leaving the lights and the oddly secure feeling of town, her back stiffened and her neck tightened. She had maybe only another mile or two left in her car before she'd have to pull over. Relief swarmed through her when he finally put his turn signal on and they turned onto what looked like a gravel path. Great, he was leading her to a point of no return. Maybe she was over imagining things, but she really had no idea who Lincoln was or why he was helping her and her family, or actually, anything else. But something about him told her he wouldn't hurt her. The gravel path twisted and turned and they finally turned onto a dirt road, which illuminated with motion lights along the drive as they continued on. The shadow of the mountain, Lynyrd Station on the Hill, loomed above them and she recognized where they were. She had no idea anyone lived here. The mountain was owned by Ford Montgomery— that fact most folks who had lived in Lynyrd Station knew. It was also a fortress of sorts, and right now, she hoped that security lent its way all the way to the bottom.

One more turn and she found Lincoln's truck parking in front of a house, difficult to see because of the darkness, and only visible from the lights on the driveway. The wood siding and long covered porch looked as if it jutted right out of the mountain and into the scene of a Norman Rockwell painting. He stepped down from his truck and she couldn't help but admire his physique. Damn, the man was almost perfect. Thick strong thighs, long legs, and that backside? Wow. He turned in her direction, and the lightness of his eyes against the dark contrast of his hair and the mountain behind him was breathtaking. He held his arm out and pointed for her to park next to his truck and she complied, eager to shut her car off and let it cool.

Once she parked, he opened the backdoor of his truck and let Abe out. He quickly ran around the back of the house and out of sight. She heard a loud splash and water running, and he chuckled.

"He just loves jumping in the river as soon as we get home. Be warned. He'll shake water all over you."

"You're on the river?" There was amazement in her voice.

"Didn't you recognize where we were headed?"

"Not really. Not until we pulled into the driveway. I was focused on other things, I guess."

True to Lincoln's warning, Abe ran toward them and stopped between them before commencing to shake water from his fur and over both of them in waves. Despite herself, she squealed and Lincoln laughed. "Welcome to Winter Valley, come on in."

He turned to walk into the house and she followed, swiping water droplets from her face. Lights flicked on and she froze. The house was absolutely amazing. It exuded warmth and charm. The walls were painted in earth tones, overstuffed furniture in neutral colors, and wooden tables adorned the living room. The kitchen was just to the right of the living room and proudly displayed shiny granite countertops in a deep rich mahogany surrounded by windows on three sides.

"Home sweet home." He dropped his keys into a decorative wooden bowl sitting on a glass and metal sofa table next to the door. He stepped into the kitchen and began rinsing and refilling a water dish for Abe, then replenished his food dish before doing anything else. Walking to the refrigerator he pulled two beers from inside and turned to look at her. "I don't have wine or champagne, princess. Will beer do?"

"Beer or bourbon are my drinks of choice."

"Bourbon? Really?"

"Why is that surprising?"

He chuckled as he pulled two bourbon glasses from a cupboard above the sink and reached above the refrigerator into a cabinet and brought out a bottle of Knob Creek. Holding that up to her, she nodded and took a deep breath. His white, three-button placket shirt fit his body like a glove and was tucked into his jeans—his shapely ass begged to be squeezed. She needed a good stiff ... drink right now. Tossing her head to move her thoughts on to matters at hand, she looked into the living room and noticed the large stone fireplace with framed pictures on the mantle. Soldiers and Marines in various uniforms stood about laughing. The photos, though in color, showed a colorless place in the Middle East—nothing but the color of sand in the background and a tent to the right of the group of men. She recognized Lincoln in a few of the photos. Then she saw Dodge. They both looked a few years younger there, more than twenty or so.

She sensed him next to her before she heard him. Her

body tingled, then his masculine scent surrounded her. The feeling was electric and alive. Her nipples puckered, and she reminded herself this wasn't a booty call. It was a conversation. She needed to tell him what was going on so he'd stay safe. Then they needed to come up with a plan for her parents. That was all.

"My battle buddies." He pointed to Dodge, then another man. "Dodge and Ford, my best friends and business partners."

She leaned in to look at Ford. "I met Dodge at my parents' today, but I've only seen Ford once or twice in town and that was in passing. I know his sister Emmy, though. She's a kick-ass defense attorney."

"Yeah, so I've heard. Ford is very proud of her."

"So, Ford sold you a piece of his mountain?"

"Yep. Dodge and me both. Dodge lives on the other side of the river. We like being close, just not too close."

He chuckled and she couldn't stop looking at him.

"We started the agency just over four months ago now. I moved here six months ago, had this house built, then we got to work organizing the agency."

He handed her a bourbon and she took a sip, loving the warmth as it slid down her throat. Yeah, that was good.

"What agency?"

He turned to her, his brows furrowed, then responded, "Big Three Bounty Hunters."

She gapped at him. "What? I thought you were a cop."

"Nope. Though we're friends with Detective Rory Richards and most of Lynyrd Station PD." He pointed to a man in the picture with the tent, and then she recognized Rory. He'd worked with Lynyrd Station PD as a detective for most of his adult life. She remembered when he and Ford had come home from Saudi Arabia after Operation

Desert Storm. There had been a big parade for them as the local hometown heroes. She'd been around thirteen then. Her father was so pumped about local boys coming home. "I was a detective back home in Arkansas, but that got old after twenty years. Dodge and I came up with the idea, over beers one night, of us working with Ford. He's been bounty hunting for years. When he got Megan pregnant, he didn't want to be out on the streets anymore. So, it's been a perfect fit."

He turned to the sofa and motioned for her to sit.

"We need to talk about what you were doing at Black Gold Pawn, princess."

14

HERE GOES

L ooking into her eyes, he saw the uncertainty. He kept reminding himself that she didn't know him that well, and trust took time, but they didn't have time right now. They needed to trust each other and fast because it seemed that things were moving at lightning speed.

"I don't know where to start." She pulled her bottom lip between her teeth, and Lord help him, that was sexy. Her golden hair flowed around her shoulders like the most expensive silk. Shining where the light kissed it, it almost seemed to sparkle. The light blue of her eyes reminded him of the cerulean blue of the waters in Greece. Unable to resist touching her, he lifted her chin with gentle fingers and tilted her face up to his.

"We have to trust each other, Skye. Did you see Victor pulling into the driveway at Black Gold? He saw us there. Both of us. We need to work on what's happening around here and where you fit in before anything else happens."

Her eyes glistened, and he braced himself for tears.

Instead, she blinked rapidly, cleared her throat, and sat a bit taller.

"Today, I came to work and entered through the shipping department. What I saw scared me."

"What did you see?" He held her gaze—steady and solid.

"I saw men ... they looked like ... I saw one man pull a carpet from the back of the truck and it struck me ..." She cleared her throat again. "He looked like one of the men who pulled that poor man from the back of the pickup truck."

"Did he see you?"

She nodded and opened her mouth but no words came out.

"How do you know he saw you?" He felt her shiver and reached behind him to pull the blanket from the back of the sofa. Wrapping it around her shoulders, he pulled it together in front of her and held it closed. It was selfish on his part because he wanted to touch her, and it wasn't lost on him that his hand lay right between her soft breasts so he intended to keep it there. Was that wrong? No. Maybe. Yeah, shit, it was wrong. Slowly, he removed his hand and picked up his bourbon.

"He stopped what he was doing and smirked at me."

He let out a slow breath. This was getting more complicated by the minute.

"Do you always enter through the shipping department?"

Her eyes looked down and she made no move, no sound. "Skye?"

"I saw you walk into the building as I was pulling into the lot. I was afraid I'd get in trouble if Victor saw me talking to you, so I decided to go in the back way."

He let out a long breath. "Yeah. Shit." He rubbed the nape of his neck with his free hand and tilted his head side to side.

"So, I understand you asked Jeannine on a date." Her lip quivered slightly but she quickly sucked it in between her teeth and released it. Leaning forward, she lifted her bourbon from the coffee table and took a sip. Quickly pulling her arm under the blanket, she pulled it tight.

"First, let's take care of your comfort." Walking to his bedroom, he pulled a long-sleeved flannel shirt from the back of his closet. His first thought was the light blue in the shirt matched her eyes. Stepping into the living room, he handed her the shirt. "Why don't you put this on. It'll be easier than holding the blanket in front of you."

She stood, her svelte figure so appealing and the last thing he should be thinking about right now. To keep himself busy, he refolded the blanket as she pulled his flannel over her thin blouse. The hem on his shirt fell close to the hem of her skirt and hung loosely over her shoulders. She sighed slightly then rolled the sleeves three or four turns before sitting back down. Picking up her bourbon, she sipped the warm amber liquid and looked him directly in the eye waiting for his response to her earlier question.

"I didn't ask her on a date. I asked her out to lunch. I need to get information, and as you just mentioned, Victor doesn't want you talking to me, so I tried another approach."

Her lips formed a straight line, and honestly, he was a bit puzzled by her reaction. "Is there a problem with Jeannine?"

Her eyes locked on his. "No."

"Then I'm not sure I understand why you seem tense right now."

His phone rang and he began pulling it from his back pocket. Just before he answered, he heard her whisper, "I'm not sure either."

Seeing Rory Richards' name on the ID, he answered. "Rory. What can I do for you?"

"Jeannine Wright was killed in a car accident about two hours ago."

His head began spinning and his breathing grew choppy. "What? Are you sure it was her?"

"Yes, we've just had her family come and ID her body. She ran off the road, up on Chambers Hill. No skid marks, nothing. We're doing toxicology on her to see if she was on something, but there are also some broken lenses from a headlight that isn't hers, so right now we're operating on the premise that she was hit from behind and purposely run off the road. Who's with the Sommerses?"

"Dodge is there until I relieve him at 2:00 a.m." He looked into Skye's eyes, the worry etched in the lines around them, her brows furrowed as she stared at him waiting to hear what was happening. "Why are you asking?"

"The man killed in their field is our undercover operative hired from GHOST, Jake Masters. We've been able to confirm it. If they saw Skye, she's on their radar and her parents may be by association. We'll need to make more permanent plans for them."

"I'll take care of it. I have an idea."

Quickly filling Skye in on his phone call, he tried reassuring her they'd be fine, but the worry on her face broke his heart.

"I have to go to my parents' house."

"Not now, you don't, and not alone. Your car isn't in any condition to make the trip and you can't be out there alone. Think of Jeannine."

She swiped across her face with the pads of her fingers, rubbing under her tired eyes. Once again he braced himself for tears, and once again, she surprised him with none.

Pulling his phone up, he touched Dodge's number and looked Skye in the eyes. Her hands reached for his hand laying on his leg, and he squeezed her fingers in his, trying to ignore the thrill that raced through his body at touching her.

"Dodge, listen, I need you to have the Sommerses pack up clothes, Jeff's medicines, and special food for a long stay. They aren't safe at the farm anymore, and I'm bringing them to Ford's for a while. We'll be there in a few hours."

Ending his call, he squeezed her hand. "You'll stay here with me."

"What? I ..." He watched her face as she wrestled with the decision so he decided to make it easier.

"I have a spare bedroom and plenty of security. I get a text and know when anyone is coming up the driveway. I have cameras all along the drive, alarms, bulletproof windows, and protection. You'll be safe here and your parents will be safe at Ford's. Plus, Megan is a nurse, so she'll be able to help with your father. Except lifting him, but Ford can help with that."

"Why are you so interested in helping us?"

Heaving out a breath, he decided to be honest. "It started as a job, but it's becoming much more."

Leaning in slowly, he allowed her time to back away or stop him. When her soft hand pulled from his, he froze.

Then her hand cupped his nape and pulled him to her, locking their lips together. She tasted like the bourbon she'd just swallowed and she felt like paradise. Her supple lips molded to his in the most perfect way. Tilting his head, he tested her lips with his tongue and was thrilled when her lips parted for him. Tasting her mouth, sliding his tongue along hers, it threatened to consume him. He drove his hands into her hair and held her close. A small whimper escaped her throat, and he captured it, wanting more. So much more.

Scooting closer to him, he dropped his arms and wrapped them lower on her body, pulling her tightly to him, eager to feel her breasts pressed into his chest. One swift lift, and he had her straddling his lap, her tight skirt riding high on her thighs. His hands cupped her firm ass and pulled her against him, the rigidness of his cock eager to feel her body. Her warmth quickly framed him and his breathing kicked up ten notches to hyperdrive. He'd been wondering what she'd feel like pulled tightly to him, but even his dreams hadn't come close to this.

The beeping from his phone alerted him to someone coming up the driveway, and it took his brain several moments to register what that meant. He froze and pulled his mouth from hers, whispering, "Someone's coming, princess."

She jumped from his lap and smoothed her skirt down, covering those glorious legs of hers. But the sight of her standing in his big flannel shirt and her work skirt peeking from the bottom did as much to him as that kiss had.

15

SO LONG SOMMER'S DREAMS

Was she crazy? Yep, she was crazy. That had to be it. With all of the crap floating around them, she was straddling Lincoln's lap and pushing herself into him like a wanton fool. She was the witness to a murder—of an undercover agent, no less. Her friend, Jeannine, was now dead, and she and her parents were in danger. The last thing she should be doing is falling for her protector. What a cliché she was.

The knock on the door startled her, but Lincoln chuckled. "It's Ford." Looking at his phone, he turned it to her, and she could see the camera outside zooming in on Ford.

Watching Lincoln's purposeful stride as he opened the door to let his friend inside was a pleasure.

They greeted each other, then Ford focused those dark eyes on her and her heart picked up a notch. She didn't remember him looking so stern and scary, though she'd really only seen him from afar.

"Nice to meet you, Skye. Ford Montgomery." Holding his hand out to shake hers, she leaned forward and grasped his firmly remembering her father always said to make a great impression with a strong handshake. It must have worked because he grinned, and suddenly he didn't look so stern. He was downright handsome. Whoa.

Lincoln hustled them into the kitchen to sit at the table, while he began pulling items from the refrigerator. She rushed over to him. "Please, let me do this for you."

His smile was worth all of this—almost. "Thanks, princess. Dig around in there and just throw a few things on a plate that we can snack on."

She busied herself with preparing something for them to eat as they discussed her parents' situation and what they could do for them all. Proud that she'd pulled together a nice tray of cheeses, meats, and olives, she set it on the table then looked at Lincoln. "Plates?"

"Third cabinet on the right."

Pulling three plates from the cabinet, she set them in front of the men, then sat next to Lincoln. He stood and pulled three beers from the fridge and plopped them down on the table before digging into the food. She glanced at the clock above the stove and saw that it was just past eight o'clock. He probably hadn't eaten since lunch and was starving.

Ford downed a cracker loaded with cheese and meat then began the conversation. "I have Falcon's room ready for the Sommerses. There's a bathroom and the laundry room down there, plenty of light, and we know how much security. Plus, Megan's a nurse, so she can help with Jeff, except for the lifting. She's due to have the baby in two months and I don't want her overdoing it." He ended with plopping another loaded cracker into his mouth as if that was that. But then those dark eyes landed on her and he asked, "Is that good with you?"

Swallowing his loaded cracker and taking a long swig of his beer, Lincoln turned toward her and waited for her response.

"Yes, Lincoln just explained it all to me, and I thank you and Megan for your hospitality."

He chuckled. "Truth be told, she's anxious to have someone else in the house to talk to. I think she's tired of spending her days and nights with only me."

Aww, cute. "I doubt that. Emmy told me you two were inseparable."

Ford looked surprised. "How do you know Emmy?"

She smiled remembering Emmy, her long dark hair always in some messed up do, because honestly, the girl could not sit down. "We went to school together. We did lose touch through college and then we both got married and Emmy began having babies. You know, life and all."

He nodded his head but said nothing more.

She turned her head to look at Lincoln and her tummy flopped when she saw he was watching her intently. "Where did you go to college?"

Inhaling, she leaned into her chair. "I went to Colorado, graduated from the University of Denver. Got married. Got divorced, I came back home and then Daddy had his accident, so now I help with the farm."

Ford's phone rang and he quickly pulled it from his pocket. His shoulders relaxed as he saw who was on the other end of the line, and he quickly said, "I was worried it would be Megan needing help. It's Jared, so I'll go in the office."

He left the room and Lincoln asked, "How long were you married?"

Turning to face him fully, she looked him in the eye and responded, "I was married for three years. I was young, fresh out of college and had my first big job in Colorado for a global manufacturer of office furniture. I felt as if I could do anything and everything. I met one of the sales associates at the company. He was handsome, bright, funny, and flattering. We married after dating only briefly, then he quit his job and let me support us. I had to get a second job because it's expensive to live in Denver. He picked our condo before we married, and it was pricey. Then I found out what he did all day and evening while I was working my ass off. He was entertaining women. In my house. In my bed. I divorced him, sold the condo, found a nice little apartment I could afford on my own and learned as much as I could learn at work. But, after a few years, I missed my family and with all of my siblings living a distance away, I didn't want my parents to be alone. I came home and not long after, well, you know."

That was a lot of information to spew out. But, whew, it felt good to let it all out. She hadn't picked up with many of her girlfriends since she'd come home, and she realized now that she'd had no one to talk to about anything. "Sorry, I guess that was a bit of an info dump."

He chuckled and it sounded good. Warm. Happy. "Not to worry, sometimes you just need to get things out there."

Then her stomach flipped and she knew she had to ask the question. "Have you ever been married?"

Setting his bottle quietly on the table, he nodded. "Yep. I married Jenny, a gal I met after my first stint in the Army. I came home and thought I was done with Army life. I met her and I was blown away. Beautiful, sophisticated, definitely upper class, and too good for me, but she was interested. We married quickly and then my story is much like yours. I ended up having to work my tail off to pay for the expensive tastes she had. We couldn't eat burgers and drink beer; we had to have prime rib and champagne. We couldn't buy clothes at any store. We had to fly to some posh place she'd found out about and spend thousands of dollars on clothes, shoes, and accessories. When I put my foot down on the spending, she packed her expensive bags and found someone who could afford her. I went back into the Army, and that's where I met Ford and Dodge."

Dang it, he was so damned handsome. Big, strong, and secure in his actions and thoughts. He wasted no time taking charge—with her dad, her, the whole situation. He made plans to keep her parents safe and he was doing the same for her. The trouble was, at this point, she had nothing to offer him. She would likely lose her job, probably already had. Now it was unsafe to go to work. Limitless was into something bad and authorities would likely shut them down. So, that left her unemployed and with a failing farm on her hands to boot. He'd certainly think she was just like Jenny, needing his money.

But gosh, if only she could see her way clear to offer Lincoln something, she'd love to explore what they had together. It was impossible to deny she was growing feelings for him. Her jealousy told her that much. Since she'd gotten divorced, she hadn't been on a single date.

First in Colorado, she was licking her wounds and trying to get her head on straight. She'd gone a whole two years thinking all men sucked. Her brother, Logan, straightened her out on that when he'd come to visit her on leave. By that time, she was skittish and worked so much she had little time to date. Then, she moved home. Knowing all the men in town did nothing to help that, she'd either grown up or gone to school with most of the eligible men in Lynyrd Station, and she had no interest in any of them. Plus, she had shit to sort out with her parents' farm. So, her personal life had taken a big backseat to everything else. Then she'd gotten what she thought was her dream job and maybe the opportunity to travel with this company; it seemed as if things would change. She made decent money but not enough to pay all the bills at home and still save a ton.

Now though, she found herself fascinated by dark-framed gray eyes and a deep throaty voice, and her mind wondered if there could be more. Maybe thinking she wanted a suit-wearing business type man wasn't really what she wanted at all. Maybe, just maybe, God was finding a way to show her what she needed and that turned out to be what she wanted? Gosh, there were so many what ifs.

She watched Lincoln now, his belt on, shoes neat and clean. And dang, but the tiny dark hairs poking from the top of his shirt made her tummy flip. His thick neck smoothed into broad shoulders, and his appeal didn't stop there. The way he was with her father and mother was simply dream worthy.

"Skye, let me show you where you'll sleep. When it's safe, we'll stop by your apartment and pick up some clothes for you to wear."

When she stood, she realized her knees were shaking, her head spun, and her breathing was shallow. This was all happening, all of this. It was a dream or a nightmare, depending on your point of view. He held his hand out for her to take, and the instant they touched, the sparks flew up her arm and raced around her body like tiny flames licking her most personal spots.

Walking down a short hallway, he pointed to one room which he used as an office. Ford sat at the desk still on the phone and jotting something on a notepad. They continued on to the next room, which was a lovely neutral-colored room, with a geometric comforter on the bed in tans and coppers. It felt warm and cozy. "This is your room."

Moving ahead of her, he walked to the window and showed her the locks. "These are bulletproof windows, and the locks can only be opened from the inside. As soon as a window is opened ..."He tugged it up an inch and a beeper went off. "You'll hear that sound. This is on all the windows and all the doors." He pushed the window down, turned the lock in place, then twisted the wand at the left to close the blinds.

He stepped to two doors, side by side. "This is the closet." He opened to show her a fairly spacious walk-in closet, mostly empty. "And this is your bathroom." As he opened this door, he stepped inside and flipped a switch. The gorgeous tan and copper tiles glistened in the light and the deep brown tiled floors were clean and perfect. She hadn't stayed in a place like this since she'd lived in Colorado, and even her condo, which was pretty darn nice, wasn't quite this nice, but it was all she could afford.

"Wow, this is beautiful."

His smile added a new light to the room and she stood transfixed at the sight before her. This handsome man, taking care of her, and seemingly happy that she approved of his home.

"Did you decorate this house? Design it?"

He chuckled. "I designed it—the layout --- but my sister, Josie, came and decorated it."

Turning around to get the full view, she sighed. "You both did a fantastic job with it."

"Thank you. Follow me." He took her hand and led her

out of this room and to one just across the hall. "This is my room, and if you need anything, I'll be right here."

The masculine feel of his room was much like him. Strong, but neat and tidy. No clothing out of place, a big wooden headboard made from barn boards and metal adorned one wall. It fit him, this old world, new world. Simple ... yet not.

"You've done a fabulous job with your home, you should be very proud." Why were her cheeks burning?

"Thank you. We'd better go and move your parents. But first ..." He pulled her into his strong beefy arms and the cocoon he wrapped around her felt like nothing ever had. When his lips touched hers, a flash of heat fanned into a flame inside her body. She could feel the flush spread across her chest and into her belly. Then lower. Right. There.

Her arms circled his waist and her hands fanned across his back, feeling solid strength under his shirt. Damn.

He pulled back and held her face between his large hands as he stared into her eyes. She could have stood there for hours encased in his arms, staring at this gorgeous man who was now her protector and becoming so much more.

"Are you two going to get hot and sweaty or come and help move Skye's parents?"

16

BRIAN

Buzzkill. Right now, Ford, his best friend, was a major buzzkill. And his body was indeed buzzing. Skye had been tantalizing from the moment he first saw her, but she was quickly edging her way into his entire life. Funny thing? He didn't mind. Not one bit.

"Ready?"

Nodding her head but saying nothing told him so much more than words could. She'd dealt with all of this drama with the strength and dignity of the strongest warrior. She'd shouldered an immense burden, and where her siblings were was beyond him. According to the pictures he'd seen hanging on the walls in the Sommers' home, she was the baby of four, so everything seemed to fall to her.

Turning, but taking her hand in his, he led her out the bedroom door and to the living room where Ford stood with a smirk on his damned face. "Not a word," he warned his friend and was grateful all he got in return was a big grin.

Ford turned and stepped out the front door, and he and Skye followed behind. He told Abe to stay and felt bad at the sadness in his loyal boy's eyes. Abe usually went everywhere with him.

"Aww, he's so sad. Can't he come?" Skye's eyes were locked on Abe, and darn it, his heart restricted, then seemed to grow a thousand times.

"We may need the room to put things in the back of the truck."

She giggled and wasn't that the best sound in the world? "Linc, I've seen the back of your truck. It's full of hair anyway, so you may as well let him come along. He'll be happier."

Leaning forward, he kissed her temple, and as if Abe knew what they'd been discussing, he jumped up and ran to Skye, pressing his head against her leg. Lucky boy.

"All right, buddy, let's go." Abe bounced out the door, tail wagging so hard he hit every surface along the way with it. Opening the backdoor for Abe to jump in, he smiled then closed it. He opened the passenger door and stood transfixed as Skye had hiked up her pencil skirt hiding under his shirt to step up into the truck. He felt the twinge in his pants watching her, and his thoughts quickly ran south. How the hell would he get any sleep tonight with her across the hall from him? Last night had been hard enough.

The drive to her parents' house was revealing. Abe continued to shower her with kisses, and to his delight, she didn't get mad or grossed out but giggled and laughed and petted his head. Abe felt the same way about her that he did, and he was a bit envious that Abe got to have so much of her attention, but his turn would come. He knew that now. He'd help her family out when they got the

Santarinos behind bars, he'd explore what this thing growing between them was.

Pulling to a stop in her parents' driveway, he commanded Abe, "*Bliebe*." He unbuckled his seat belt and looked over at Skye who was suddenly very still and quiet. She stared out the windshield at the shrubbery in the front of the house, and he could see her pulse racing in her neck.

"What is it, Skye?"

"I saw something in the bushes. I thought I did. I don't see anything now." She shook her head as if to clear it then turned to him. "My imagination is getting the better of me, I'm afraid."

"Maybe not. Stay put for a minute." Jumping from the truck, he met Ford at the hood. "Skye thought she saw something."

"Okay, I'll go and check it out. You take her inside."

"Maybe I should send Abe in first. He can ferret out anyone, and if not, he'll scare the bastards away if there's anyone skulking around."

Ford glanced at the front of the house, then nodded.

Having another thought, Lincoln said, "Let's do this. Point your truck's headlights to the front of the house from this angle. I'll pull down the drive just a bit and shine on the front of the house from that direction, then I'll let Abe out. If anyone is back there, they'll be blinded by the headlights and scared by Abe, so we'll be able to grab them for sure."

Ford nodded and slapped him on the shoulder. "You're always thinking, man. I'll call Dodge and let him know what's up."

Hopping back into his truck, he backed down the driveway while telling Skye what they were going to do, adding, "I need you to duck, Skye, in case they have a gun."

"Oh my God, I didn't think of that. My parents—"

"Ford's calling Dodge and will get them into an interior room. Hopefully, it'll be nothing, but we need to be prepared."

The fear on her face made him sorry once again that she was going through all of this, and if there were any way at all to shield her from it, he surely would. Turning his truck slightly, he pointed the headlights at the front of the house as Ford did the same from the side.

Stepping from the truck, he opened the backdoor, petting Abe's head and commanded, "*Suche*," which meant search.

Abe, fast as lightening, jumped from the truck and ran to the shrubbery, disappearing into the thick of it. Rustling could be heard, thrashing, then Abe began barking loudly. Lincoln ran to his dog, knowing barking meant he'd found something—or someone. Pressing his back against the wall of the house, he edged his way in behind the foliage with Abe, and shuffled along the wall until he reached his boy. "*Ruhig*," he yelled.

Abe quieted, and he pulled his phone up and turned on the flashlight app. Shining his light in the direction Abe pointed, he saw a man lying in the bushes, head bloodied, eyes large in fear. "What's your name?"

The man never moved his eyes from Abe. "Brian."

"What are you doing here, Brian?"

"I ... I saw strange trucks coming and going from here and heard about the murder in the field so I came to see what was going on. I was hit on the back of the head." He touched his head with a shaking hand, then finally looked at him. "I don't know how I got in the bushes. I was trying to get out when your dog damn near killed me."

"Hardly." Lincoln clicked his tongue and Abe backed away. Pushing his way from the shrubbery, he stood just on the outside of the landscaping and Abe came to heel at his side. "Were you alone?"

"Clearly not, someone hit me."

Beginning to get irritated, Lincoln lowered his voice. "Were you alone when you came here?"

"Ye ... yes."

Turning in Ford's direction, he yelled, "I've got one man, injured. Another one lurking." He shone his flashlight in the vicinity, and upon taking a closer look, he saw a shovel laying a few steps away. He picked it up to look it over and found blood along the edge.

He heard his friend coming around the opposite side of the house, and he continued to stare at Brian.

Ford reported, "I didn't find anyone around. Let's get everyone inside. Lynyrd Station PD will be here soon."

Brian struggled to sit up, winced, grabbed one of the sturdier bushes and weakly said, "I've got to get going."

Ford chuckled. "Why would you want to leave before the cops get here? You should file a report."

"Nah. I just need ... I've got to get going. I'll call them in the morning."

Lincoln couldn't stop staring at this idiot. He claimed he'd been hit in the head, yet he wasn't willing to file a report with the cops, and just what the fuck was he doing lurking around here?

"Nah," he said, mimicking Brian's speech. "I think you need to come inside and wait for the cops. They're friends of ours, and they're thorough and friendly. You'll like them." Hearing his truck door open then close, he glanced over to see Skye walking toward them. "Princess, stay there," he yelled, pleased that she halted but not pleased when Brian took that moment to slip around the opposite side of the house at a full run. Ford took off after him from across the lawn and Abe whimpered. He wanted to run. "*Suche*," he told his pup and off he went.

Not two minutes later the sound of a four-wheeler could be heard heading away from them faster than he should be going in the dark through a field. It was too dark to follow him; that would have to be something to investigate tomorrow.

He stepped up to Skye, let out a long slow breath, and looked deeply into her eyes. "I asked you to stay in the truck and get your head down. Instead, you get out of the truck and put yourself in danger. What the fuck, Skye?"

She blanched at the reprimand, then her shoulders hunched in defeat. "I wasn't thinking clearly. I thought you found who or what was in the bushes."

"We didn't know there weren't more people here." He scraped his hand through his hair and rubbed the nape of his neck. "Princess, you've got to listen to me when I ask you to do something. I can't keep you safe if you don't."

She nodded, then wrapped her arms around herself in a protective gesture. He felt bad for scolding her, so he decided to let it go for now. "Let's get going. This makes it even clearer that moving your parents is of utmost importance."

17

THE FIRST TIME

2:00 a.m.

Between discussing Brian with Lynyrd Station PD and waiting for them to investigate the area and organizing the Sommerses' belongings, it had taken them more than five hours to get home. The medical paraphernalia alone took forever. Monitors, walkers, toilet and shower aids, special pillows and that recliner Jeff had grown so accustomed to. Then the medications, good grief, there were so many. One of the things Jeff needed more than anything was a new doctor.

He'd spoken to both Skye and Megan once they'd gotten to the mountain top home Ford and she shared. He asked Megan to look through Jeff's medications and make sure he actually needed them all. Being in his early fifties, he shouldn't need all of those. Sure, he'd broken bones in his back and had to have surgery, but that was more than a year ago, and he should have been weaning off most of those by now. Between addiction and improper medical attention, there were many things that could be a factor here. It was time to dig into it. Luckily, Skye readily agreed with the discussion and Megan's assistance in helping to solve some of her father's issues. Once she'd catalogued each prescription, she'd help Jeff find a new doctor and try and sort all of that out.

Feeling bone weary and edgy were a dangerous combination. He wanted to crash, but Skye's proximity and all the events of the past few days kept him too wired to sleep. He flopped on the sofa, listening to the water running as Skye showered in the room a few feet down the hall. His mind continually wandered to the water sliding down her body and his dick liked those thoughts. A lot.

Needing to do something to relieve his stress and the blood running south of his brain, he went into his office and flipped open his laptop. One thing for sure, Skye couldn't go back to work at Limitless. No doubt in his mind the Santarinos had Jeannine killed. Skye filled him in on the happenings at the office and that Victor had been pissed that Jeannine had lunch with him. That meant Skye wasn't safe anymore either.

Searching through databases on the Santarinos, he began looking for anything that connected them with the pawn shop. They were very good at covering their tracks, but one sure thing, his friend, Jared Timm, would have more info than anyone ever dreamed. Jared, forever a conspiracy theorist, had amassed a database of useful information. In the Army, he'd been their hacker, able to get into anyone's computer network and ferret out information. As a private citizen, he was much more useful— he didn't have government restrictions placed on him now. The average person would be horrified at the places Jared's spider network traveled. Right now, he was traveling into Santarino territory for him.

Entering his private password, he grimaced at how much this was costing them. Jared was good, but he didn't come cheap. Clicking on their code name for the Santarinos—Columbus—he chuckled. The Italians were so proud of their brethren, Christopher Columbus. Long lists of information began populating his screen. Names, birthdates, social security numbers, addresses, credit card purchases, bank records, financial and real estate holdings. The Santarinos were a busy family.

Along with the family members, Mangus, and his younger brother, Victor, they had a younger sister, Giovanna, their father, Giovanni, and mother, Stephania. Real estate holdings all over the world, in each of their names filled his screen.

The Santarino wives also had real estate holdings, though mostly in Italy and Europe. What was most notable was that Mangus Santarino's wife, Sofia, owned the real estate in Lynyrd Station. Not that it was a big deal who owned it, but interesting that Mangus seemed to have some interest in Skye, according to the picture he'd seen and Jeanine, and yet his wife owned the real estate that hired Skye. Maybe that was just a hint of jealousy showing through.

Scrolling down the page, finally something of complete interest caught his eye. Butch Ariens' name. In the column next to his name, -$143,908.00. Butch *did* owe them money. He clicked on Butch's name and a spreadsheet populated his screen, showing what appeared to be payments or credits to his account over the course of the past few months. Nothing before Limitless came to Lynyrd Station.

A blow dryer sounded from the room directly behind his office, and he imagined those golden strands hanging over her bare shoulders and curling around her full breasts. This thought tightened his pants and forced him to stand. Better think about crime families and murder again.

Walking to the kitchen, he pulled a beer from the fridge and downed a good half of it before taking a breath. Deciding to let the information he'd found roll around in his head for a while, he headed back to his office to shut his computer down. Before making it to the office door, Skye's bedroom door opened and a fairy princess walked out. Wearing cut-off denim shorts and a thin, soft-looking T-shirt, she was a vision. Her long, toned, tanned legs were perfection in the flesh, her bright pink toenails an excellent touch to the end of each toe. His eyes traveled all the way down her body, then back up, taking in every facet of the vision standing before him. His eyes stopped at her breasts, seeing one of those envious locks of hair expertly swooped around a firm breast and leaving a dampness just below it. What he wouldn't give to be that curl. Continuing his journey, his heart pumped wildly as he saw her swallow, then his vision landed on her eyes, which were locked on him.

"You look fresh and ... perfect." Lame, but his brain wasn't working just now.

"Thank you. I'm so glad I had some clothes stashed at my parents' house."

Tucking her hands in the front pockets of her shorts pushed her breasts out farther, and Lord help him, his throat constricted, and his pants grew tighter.

He stood stone still, unsure what to do and not trusting his body to do what it was supposed to do, cause dammit, right now it knew what it wanted to do, and that had nothing to do with security or helpfulness. Not to Skye, anyway. It would help him a lot. Maybe he needed to have sex with her to clear his head. No, that was stupid and so full of clichés. He clenched his jaw tighter.

His balls tightened up into his body just a bit when she stepped forward toward him and her fresh-from-the-shower scent filled his nostrils. Unable to organize a clear thought in his head, he continued to stare—dumbfounded. When her hands touched his chest and slid up to his shoulders, he knew his resolve was crumbling. He didn't care either. If she wanted him, he sure as fuck wouldn't deny her, because his thoughts had been consumed with her since the first moment he'd laid eyes on her.

"Lincoln." She whispered it, and hearing his name had never sounded like music before. But, her siren song was playing now, and he would happily fall for it.

Wrapping his arms around her, he pulled her into his body. Her breasts smashed against his chest and his cock throbbed. Her lips turned up to his, and he claimed her mouth fully. His tongue plunged deeply into her mouth; he tasted every inch of her. Playing his lips softly over hers, his mind blanked out everything but Skye. His hand slid up her back, pulling her into his body and he heard her whisper, "Perfect."

Yep, sure was. Her tongue matched his as she explored his mouth, sliding along his, a perfect erotic dance. One of her hands slid into his hair and held his head in place as she rose on her toes to get closer. Sliding his hand down to her ass, he bent his knees then hoisted her up his body, thrilled when her sexy legs swiftly wrapped around him.

"Your room or mine?" It was torture just getting those words out, but when she responded, "Yours," his cock hardened to steel, and he had to work hard to concentrate on not tripping over his feet to get them the few feet to his room.

Placing a knee on his bed, he slowly lowered her to the mattress, pulling away only long enough to set the remainder of his beer on the nightstand. When he turned back to her, he was thrilled to see she'd already removed her T-shirt. His knee moved between her legs and slid to her warmth. Using that leverage, he moved a hand under her back and pushed with his knee to move her up the mattress, excited when she moaned in pleasure.

Her fingers worked his belt open, quickly undoing the button at his fly and lowering his zipper. Her hand dove in and grasped his cock as much as she could in the confines of his jeans, and he lost the air in his lungs at the feel of her hand cupping him.

Sitting back briefly, he pulled his shirt off, pulled a condom from his nightstand, shucked his jeans and his briefs. Tugging her cutoffs off before rejoining her on the mattress, he enjoyed the light pink lacy bra and panties before deciding the panties, cute as they were, needed to go. Tucking fingers in on each side, he shimmied them down her long legs while she removed her bra. The light from the hallway shining in was dim, but it caressed her skin like a lover. His biggest issue now was deciding between the golden curls between her legs or those perfect nipples tightened to sharp points.

The curls won.

Dipping his head down to nuzzle along the seam of

her pussy, he inhaled the fresh scent of her mingled with the musky excitement wetting her. His tongue wet a trail along the seam from below her entrance all the way into her blonde hairs. Her breathing grew choppy, and that caused him to suck her clit into his mouth and flick it with his tongue. Her hands drove into his hair and tugged slightly while he continued to alternate between sucking and licking her. When her knees spread open wider for him, he slid a finger into her entrance, delighted when she moaned. He could hear her whisper his name as he manipulated her clit and fingerfucked her.

He heard her gasp as her orgasm hit. His finger slid out and his mouth replaced it, drinking her in. When he felt her relax slightly, he climbed up her body, made quick work of the condom, positioned his cock at her entrance, and looked into her eyes as he slowly entered her.

When her legs wrapped around him, he began a slow steady rhythm, in and out, enjoying her body, her sweet sounds of pleasure, and the heat of her body gripping his cock.

He ground against her, enjoying the sweet sounds she made each time. He held himself above her so he could watch her face the first time he came inside her. You only got one first time and he wanted to remember it. As he felt the tightening in his groin, the uncomfortableness as his balls drew up tight inside him, he increased his speed, racing to his own orgasm but wanting badly to give her another one. Pushing hard and fast, he knew he was close. He felt like a stallion racing to the finish line, the sweat on his back and chest a true testament to his effort. Grinding his hips once more into her, he clinched his jaw tighter as she finally cried out his name while she orgasmed once again and he released himself into her. With the blinding pulsing pressure flowing into her body, the only thing he could see was stars twinkling before his eyes.

Moments later, after their hearts beat a normal rhythm, he pulled the covers down. "Climb in, princess. I'll go shut off the lights and be right back."

Watching her snuggle in, a soft smile on her face, he donned his briefs and made his way to the kitchen, flipping off the lights, checking the locks on the doors and then moving through the rest of the house. Entering his office, he noticed an email from Jared. Curiosity got the better of him, so he clicked it open and froze when he saw a picture of Skye.

18

DOUBT

The light filtering into the window brightened the room just enough for her to admire the setting. This room was comfortable—masculine --- but not to the point of making her feel uncomfortable and definitely not in a gross way. Lincoln was very regimented and neat. No clothes lay out of place, no dust on the surface of any of the furniture that she'd found, and she wondered if he cleaned his own place or if someone cleaned it for him.

That thought flashed to an ugly thought that what if he had someone—a female someone—in his life. She'd never asked. It was presumptuous of her to think he was interested in her and unattached. Look at the man. Any red-blooded woman would want to be attached to him. Her mother, for crying out loud, couldn't stop sounding like a teenager when he was around.

Rolling to her side, she looked at the empty spot where he'd slept beside her last night, his pillow still indented where his head lay. Her tummy came to life with butterflies. She and Lincoln had sex last night, and it was amazing. While she was taking her shower, she thought about him. Not sure how the evening would unfold, the moment happened of its own accord once she stepped from her room, and there he was.

She'd fallen asleep before he'd come back into the room, unfortunately. Snuggling into his arms would have been the perfect way to fall asleep, but apparently she'd been too tired.

That brought the flood of all that was going on to her thoughts, and unfortunately, she'd not had enough coffee to deal with those thoughts.

Pulling the covers back, she slid from the bed, her toes curling into the high pile soft-as-silk carpet. Noticing Lincoln had picked up her clothing and lay it neatly on the chair in the corner brought a smile to her face. Neat and tidy.

A quick glance out the window confirmed that the pattering she heard on the roof was indeed rain. At least her car would stay cooler when she drove it home. Mental note to stop at the hardware store and pick up another jug of antifreeze.

Entering the living room, she could see into the kitchen and there he stood, looking intently out the window. His back straight, his shoulders level. In one hand was a steaming cup of coffee, and her mouth almost watered. His other hand rested on the edge of the counter on top of some papers. He must have been awake for a long while.

Continuing toward Lincoln, she felt his edginess the closer she came to him, and her stomach tightened. First glancing out the same window he stared out she saw that she was correct in the assumption that his house sat on the edge of the river at the bottom of the mountain. What a glorious sight. The water ran swiftly this morning, the rain filling it up and pushing it along its winding path faster than its usual lazy pace.

"Morning." He hadn't so much as made an acknowledgement that she was in the room, and when he didn't jump or start at her greeting, her stomach tightened into a hard ball.

"Would you like coffee?" His tone was even and detached and she was stunned to the point of muteness.

Finally, he turned to look at her, and his eyes lingered so long that self-consciousness creeped in. Absently finger combing her hair, she twisted her curls into a bun at the top of her head; pulling a clip from her purse, still tucked into the corner of the sofa where she'd left it last night, she snapped it onto her hair. Having no idea what that looked like, she finally answered his previous question.

"Yes, please, but I can get it myself."

Walking to the coffeepot on the counter behind Lincoln, she poured her coffee into a cup he'd set out for her. She turned to look at him over her shoulder. "Would you like a refill?"

"No." His flat reply once again settled hard in her stomach.

Placing the pot back in on the warmer, she turned and that's when she saw the papers on the counter were pictures. Of her. Correction, her and Mangus Santarino. The art gallery in San Diego that Limitless owned. They had an employee function there and the whole staff from Lynyrd Station had been flown down on a private jet that weekend. It had been the stuff dreams were made of.

"Why do you have these?"

"I think the better question is why are there so many pictures of you and Mangus Santarino?"

Her eyes traveled over the pictures and then she saw it. Every picture he had on the counter was of her and Mangus. No one else.

Her throat tightened up and her eyes searched for anyone else in the pictures. A hand, someone in the background, anything. "I don't know. Where did you get them?"

"Why don't you first tell me what's between you and Mangus?"

"Nothing." She stepped away from the counter and him, her head shaking and her knees as well. "He's my boss. Nothing more."

Lincoln pointed to a newspaper clipping and a picture of her and her boss. "This is from *Gornali Italiano,* a newspaper in Italy. Why in the hell would a newspaper take a picture of the two of you unless there was a story to tell?"

"We had dinner at Victoriano's in California. It's a restaurant the Santarino family owns. But we weren't alone. The whole office staff of the Lynyrd Station Limitless was there."

Lincoln's eyes looked down at the pictures, then slid back to hers. "I don't see another soul there."

"But ..." She studied the photos again, trying to find something to prove she wasn't lying.

His fingers toyed with the pictures, sliding them in front of her, one after the other. Damning pictures that looked like they were having an affair. That told a story that was a lie. "This one."

He continued to point. "How about this one?" Mangus had given a toast before the gallery opened in California for an exhibit of a local artist. The picture captured Mangus and her clinking their champagne glasses.

Her stomach threatened to lurch, and if she didn't sit soon she'd surely fall. Then she remembered the Limitless employee intranet. She managed to say, "Let me show you what these pictures really are."

She walked as fast as her shaky legs would take her to her bedroom. She grabbed her laptop case sitting on the floor next to the bed and walked back to the kitchen. Lincoln was refreshing his coffee when she set her laptop on the center island, pulled it from the case, and opened the lid. Waiting for it to boot up was painful and the room was eerily quiet, save for Abe snoring on his doggy bed in the corner of the room.

Her fingers shook as she logged into Limitless International's intranet, and she pulled up the photo album stored on the server for employees to add the pictures they'd taken of any and all events. They catalogued everything they did.

Glancing at the pictures on the counter, she pointed to one. "This one is at the California gallery event for Thomas Diego, a local artist in California who we did a private gala for ..." Tapping a couple of times on different links, she pulled up the actual picture. There she was, next to Mangus, but there were people on either side of them, and while it looked like he was looking into her eyes in the picture Lincoln had, in her picture, you could see he was looking at his assistant, Jasmine, who stood just behind her.

He leaned in and if his breathing was any indication, he was beginning to realize something was up.

Quickly clicking on another link, she pulled up the picture that had appeared in *Gornali Italiano* and showed him the full photograph. "This is the real picture of all of us at Victorianos."

She continued through all seven of the pictures he had on the counter, proving she hadn't been alone in another city having some clandestine affair with Mangus.

"Princess, I'm sorry I doubted you. These pictures are damning. Mangus is married. Who would want to harm him or you in this way?"

19

AND WHO IS THIS?

Scraping his hand through his hair for the hundredth time in this short day so far, Lincoln looked into Skye's eyes. If he were being honest with himself, she was the most beautiful woman he'd ever seen. Ever. Outward beauty was a given, but this sweet seemingly innocent woman had gotten herself into a peck of trouble. That is if a peck was a shit-ton, which in this case it was. And holy mother of ass, this was a shit-ton.

"Princess." He took a deep breath, needing to make sure his thoughts were concise on this matter, and his heart be damned, he needed to make sure his decisions were for the right reasons—not his reasons. Needing contact with her, he ran his thumb along her cheek as his fingers cupped her jaw. Soft, smooth, and slightly cool to the touch, it said everything about her. She was loyal to her family, cool under pressure, and soft and malleable to his touch. Remembering how she felt last night, his body lurched to attention, and his mind struggled to keep up. "You can't go back to work at Limitless. At least not until things get figured out. I'm sure that worries you, but I'll help you figure it out. Someone is running a smear campaign on you or Mangus or both of you. I'm not sure, but these pictures, which by the way are posted on the internet and in newspapers, are certainly trying to do something here; otherwise, why bother?"

Her teeth caught her bottom lip and pulled it into her sweet mouth. Her eyes never left his as she waited silently for his next words. "I'm also worried long term about you staying here with me. Short term it's a fantastic solution, but I've got to be out there looking for the evidence we need for so many things. Lynyrd Station PD is looking into the murder of Agent Masters, but we suspect it was your employees at Limitless who did the job. Under whose order, we don't know yet. Then there's the whole host of other issues to keep track of. Jeannine, Brian, Butch Ariens. Good God, Skye, this shithole is getting deeper by the day."

"Linc, I need to work. My parents need help. I have rent to pay, expenses, I can't ..." Her voice caught on the edge of a sob. Placing both of her hands on either side of her face, maybe as a comfort gesture, she closed her eyes and took two long deep breaths in and slowly released them. Abe must have sensed her distress and came to stand in front of her, resting his head on her knee. She seemed to regain a calmness about her, patted his head, then continued. "Okay, I have some savings, though it's dwindling fast. If we need to sell some of the land around the farm, we can do that. And the rest I'll figure out, even if I have to ask my siblings to help out."

Unable to resist this stoic princess before him, he reached out and gently pulled her to her feet, wrapping his arms tightly around her. When her slender yet strong arms wrapped around his waist, he lay his cheek on her head and inhaled her fresh citrusy scent. His heart was losing its battle to stay clear of this drama-wrapped woman. What would he do about that? When this was all over, the very thing that brought them together would be gone, and then, if they found they had nothing in common, she'd walk away. That would be a different battle to fight.

Lifting his head and swallowing, he took a step back to put some distance between them. He couldn't think straight when she was wrapped in his arms. "Okay, princess. Let's get ready to head on up to Ford and Megan's. You can visit with your parents while Ford, Dodge and I discuss long-term strategies."

"You know I appreciate all you're doing for my family and me, but honestly, that just sounded a bit like, be a good little girl and let the men do all the work. I'm a big girl, Lincoln, and I want to be involved in saving myself."

"I didn't mean to ..." His words floated back to his brain. He guessed they did sound a bit like he was talking over her and taking charge. He didn't know any other way.

"Okay, look, I've been at this type of work for a long time. I do what I do. I take charge. It's never steered me wrong."

"I'll accept that as an explanation. But I meant what I said."

"So did I. And you should call into work and tell them you won't be there today. Good thing is it's Friday, so we'll have a couple of days to figure some of this out before you have to do anything permanent." Lightening the moment, he winked at her, and that earned him a smile. He'd take it.

He heard the shower turn on and decided to make breakfast to keep his mind off the visions he'd had last night. Freshening his cup, his phone beeped, alerting him to someone in the backyard. Looking out his window, he saw a man pulling a canoe onto the shore at the edge of his property. He watched as the man looked from side to side and gathered a few things from the bottom of his canoe. Before he knew what the man was stuffing into a backpack, Abe flew out the doggy door and ran a straight line to the man.

Hearing Abe barking and snarling, the surprised man twisted to see his enemy running toward him at break-neck speed, teeth bared. Reaching into his vest, he tried pulling what looked like a gun, but Abe jumped into the air and knocked the man over, the heavy object flying from his hand and landing in the water.

Lincoln ran out the door and rounded the side of the house, impressed with his boy as he stood over the man, barking nonstop. Each time the man tried to move, Abe took hold of his clothing and shook him until he froze once again.

"*Bliebe.*" He halted Abe's barking. The man never took his eyes from Abe as he slowly began pushing himself away from the dog with his feet. Abe lunged again, and Lincoln grinned at his pup's tenaciousness before halting him.

"Halt!" he commanded Abe.

The man lying on the ground grunted something under his breath, and Lincoln, knowing full well Abe had this under control, searched the area with his eyes to see the canoe held duct tape, rope, a knife, and other nefarious materials that bespoke of a kidnapping and not a fishing expedition.

"Who are you and what do you want?" he bellowed.

The man's eyes darted back and forth between him and Abe, probably assessing which of them posed the greater risk.

"Make him leave me alone."

Standing straighter, Lincoln's response was to cross his arms and wait him out. The man moved to sit and Abe growled, halting his progress briefly while he determined his best move.

Deciding not to toy with the man any longer, he pulled his phone from his pocket and held the nine on his keypad, dialing the local 911 operator. Quickly giving his address, he also said, "Tell Detective Richards to come on out as well."

Finishing his call, he pocketed his phone, his eyes never leaving the man lying on the ground. Then it hit him. He'd seen this man before. Delivering pizza to Butch Ariens last night.

"I asked you once before to tell me who you were. I'll give you another chance at it."

"Fuck you. You aren't going to do anything to me now that you have the cops on the way."

"Suit yourself. I might not. Can't vouch for Abe here though. Sometimes he just has a mind of his own. And he just hates pizza delivery boys, trespassers, and criminals— all of which you are, so ..."

Feeling brave enough to sit up, the man spat on the ground and sneered at Lincoln.

"Shame about your gun flying off into the river."

That didn't get him a response. His phone chirped,

and the man tried a different tactic. "If you need to take that, go ahead. I'm good."

Lincoln chuckled and continued to stare, which caused his captive to squirm. Another beep on his phone, and he raised his voice, never looking away from his prey. "I'm in the back."

20

HERE WE GO

"Well, I'm not a damsel in distress. I won't be. I won't be treated like one." Hands planted firmly on her hips, she stood facing Ford, Lincoln, and Dodge. Her parents sat at the counter, their coffee growing cold, having already said their piece, to which she had scolded them for forcing her to be complacent and wait while the men rescued them. Megan stood across the counter from her parents, her belly large with child, a smile on her gorgeous face and slowly clapped.

"Well said, Skye."

Ford glanced back at his wife, shook his head, and then looked at Lincoln who had a scary scowl on his face.

Dodge, handsome as he was with his sandy hair and green eyes, stood, crossed his massive arms over his chest, and proudly announced, "We don't involve our women in our business."

To which three pairs of female eyes lanced him with daggers so sharp and powerful he visibly cowed to sit between his friends.

Megan apparently deciding she'd held her tongue far too long, waddled around the counter and stood next to her husband, but her eyes never left Dodge's.

"First of all, 'your women,'"— she made finger quotes — "aren't helpless imbeciles." Pointing a finger at Dodge, she then continued, "And as I look around this room, I don't see a woman that is yours."

That earned her a chuckle from Ford, to which she turned to face her husband. "Stop talking about Skye and her parents as if they aren't in the room."

Then she turned her green eyes, which Skye admitted were the prettiest shade of green she'd ever seen, toward her. "Skye, honey, if you want to be involved in helping get you and your parents to safety, you need to speak up and tell these Neanderthals what you want to do to help."

That earned her a few murmurs and a couple of grunts from said Neanderthals, but Megan held the room, and to her credit, they were listening.

"Now, let's begin again, and how about you all try to remember who you're talking about and how they play a very important role in their own safety. These are people who we all care about—not a bunch of dogs." Turning to the rug in front of the fireplace and Abe whose head popped up from his nap to stare, she replied, "Sorry, buddy. You know what I mean."

His tail thumped a couple of times before he dropped his head and resumed his nap.

Ford stood, pulled his chair away from the table a bit, then gently scooted his wife to it to sit. "Don't get so worked up, Meg."

"Ford, I'm—"

"I'm not telling you what to do, I'm taking care of you and Eggplant."

The puzzled looks around the table were comical to see. Then Skye's mom started laughing, and her dad followed suit.

Ford shrugged and told the confused men at the table, "The baby's the size of an eggplant this week."

He pulled another chair from against the wall and sat next to his wife. Lincoln turned to look at her and softly asked, "Would you please join us to discuss how we should handle getting you and your parents to Jared's for safekeeping?"

Dodge mumbled, "Geez."

Lincoln ignored him. There. That was better. His earnest look made her smile, and then her cheeks burned because she realized she'd probably just stirred up a bit of a fuss while these guys were just trying to help her and her parents out. But, she didn't know how she'd repay them, and each passing hour felt like she was drowning further in indebtedness.

Two hours later, the plan was hatched, and now she had to admit, she was scared out of her mind. What if she flubbed up? This wasn't the type of work she did. But mostly she was thinking, *What the fuck have I gotten myself into?*

"Princess, are you ready?" Lincoln's deep, sexy voice floated over her like a warm blanket on a cold day. Locking eyes with him, she tried to smile, but it probably looked more like a grimace. So, she nodded.

He chuckled. "You can change your mind."

"No. I don't want to. I'll admit I'm scared. I don't want to let you and your friends down, and I don't want to get my parents hurt or killed."

He reached forward and tucked his fingers into the pockets of her jeans and pulled her to him, kissed her forehead, and wrapped his arms around her. The warmth of his body pressed to hers was like a soothing balm. She closed her eyes to enjoy this warmth because she didn't know how long it would be before she felt it again. She sent up a silent prayer that this would work.

After a few glorious moments, he stepped back and quietly requested, "Tell me what you're doing."

"Okay. Mom and Dad will be riding with me. I'm driving them down the mountain in Megan's SUV, and we're going to the Copper Cup. I'm to park as close as I can, and we're to go inside, head straight to the back and into the kitchen, through the backdoor and into Ford's brother, Dawson Montgomery's, plumbing truck in the back. He'll then drive us to Jared's where we'll stay in his underground bunker until you come and get us. Hopefully that'll only be a day, maybe two. We have dad's medicine packed, and Jared has a recliner for dad to sit in. We'll manage.

His smile was perfect. Honestly, she could stare at him all day. Right now, she'd prefer that to anything else, especially being responsible for getting her parents down the mountain and into the Copper Cup without incident.

"Yes. And if you feel as though you're in trouble before you get to the restaurant, what do you do?"

She cleared her throat of the knot that was forming. "Mom will call the cops, and I keep driving around until I see them coming. We're not to get out of the car without one of you or the police with us."

"By golly, you've got this."

"Okay. And Dodge will be at the Copper Cup as a customer in case we need help inside. And you'll be in town, watching the Black Gold Pawn Shop. And Ford will be sitting out by Limitless watching for any unusual activity to see if they're on to any of us."

"Perfect."

Ford called out. "All right, let's get rolling. Skye, your parents are in Megan's SUV waiting for you. I'm heading out now. Dodge is already gone."

Standing in front of Ford and Megan's fireplace, Abe began pacing. He knew he was going to work, and her stomach twisted tightly into a ball. Lincoln kissed her lips softly but firmly enough to convey possession. Or maybe it was fear. His hands framed her face, but his lips lingered just a bit more. Pulling away, she felt the immediate loss and wished she could take all of her bravado back. She wasn't a mercenary kind of girl. She was a farm girl turned corporate girl turned hunted girl. She liked the last one least of all.

"Follow directions, drive carefully, be safe, and come back to me, princess."

Her heart began thumping so hard she thought she'd become dizzy. Oh my God. "Come back to me."

Her knees grew weak. Sucking in a deep, strong breath, she looked into his eyes and hoped it wouldn't be the last time. "You come back to *me*, Lincoln Winter."

His hand rubbed at the nape of his neck and she tilted her head to the side. "Are you nervous or irritated?"

"What do you mean?"

She pointed to his hand at the back of his neck. "You rub the back of your neck when you're irritated or nervous. Which is this?"

He dropped his hand onto her shoulder and then cupped her jaw. "I'm nervous. I want you safe. All of you. I don't doubt you can do this, it's just there are many moving parts and that's when things go wrong."

She agreed with that. Giving his lips a quick peck, she tried to smile, but it was stiff.

Taking her hand, they walked to the garage door where Ford kissed Megan and then told her to lock the doors up tight. She shook her head as if she'd heard it a million times before, probably every day. Megan grabbed Skye's arm as she passed. "You've got this, Skye. I'll see you in a day or two."

The lump in her throat didn't allow her to respond, so she smiled, nodded, and hugged Megan before she continued out the door.

Lincoln opened the driver's door and held it for her until she was safely belted into the seat. He ducked his head in to glance at her parents. "See you all in a day or so. Take care." He kissed her temple then closed the door.

The garage filled with light as the door opened, and she let out a long breath. "Okay, here we go."

Thank God her parents were quiet going down the mountain. She was nervous and not used to navigating the steep mountain drive, especially in someone else's vehicle. She sure didn't need a barrage of questions right now. Her stomach could barely handle this much. At every turn she felt like she'd throw up, her heart beat erratically, and she reminded herself to stay the hell out of Lincoln's business from this point forward. She didn't know how he did it.

Finally at the county road at the bottom of the drive, she turned left, to bring them into town and silently prayed for the hundredth time she didn't screw up. Lincoln was behind her in his truck, Abe's ears next to his. Maybe Abe was watching her too; that was sweet.

The county road had light traffic on it thank goodness. Every time she met someone or another vehicle pulled from a driveway or road behind her, she could feel the sweat forming between her breasts and under her arms. She hadn't asked, but she sure hoped Jared's bunker had a shower. Glancing in her rearview mirror, she saw Lincoln flash his headlights once and pull off the county road to head to the side of town by the pawn shop. Okay, now she was on her own. That felt so sad and scary, and the crazy thought flashed through her mind that she didn't want to be without Lincoln. Not just for the security he offered, but for the man he was. He wasn't a Neanderthal. None of the guys were, but he for sure wasn't one. As her mother pointed out after her outburst, there was nothing wrong with having someone care for you and want to do anything to keep you safe. She was fortunate in that.

Glimpsing a dark blue sedan pull onto the road, she watched as it kept a bit of a distance. Inhaling and letting it out slowly, she concentrated on the road, but glanced every so often in her rearview mirror. Turning onto Shanty Road brought her one more road closer to town and within five minutes they'd be there. *Almost there*, was her new mantra.

"Why are you looking in your mirror so often, Skye? Is someone following us?"

Her mom started to turn and look, but Skye halted her. "No, don't look back. He'll see you, and then we alert him to the fact that we're watching him."

"Oh, dear," her mom mumbled. "I'm getting the phone ready."

Deciding to test the blue sedan, she turned a road sooner than she needed, but she knew this road. Her best friend from high school had lived down this road, and she'd been on it hundreds of times over the years.

Her father stiffened in the passenger seat and braced

himself with a hand on the dashboard in front of him, but to his credit, he remained quiet as a church mouse.

The sedan followed them down the road, and a hot, rock-like object formed in her stomach. Turning right and down a separate side street, she waited and focused on keeping her speed even until she saw the blue sedan follow her down that street. Turning once again, she noticed Lincoln's blue pickup behind the dark sedan and her breathing hitched. "Linc's back there now."

Honest to God, her mother sighed. Her father mumbled, "Jesus." And thankfully the SUV grew quiet again.

The convenience store at the south end of town came into view, and she decided to pull in there and see if the sedan followed. Pulling in and up to a pump, she stayed inside as Lincoln had asked her to do and watched as the sedan followed her into the station and parked at the edge of the parking lot. Lincoln pulled into the station as well and parked his truck at an angle in front of the sedan. Climbing down from his truck, he walked to the sedan and began chatting with the man inside. Skye took this as an opportunity to leave without being followed. Pulling out at a different exit from the one she pulled into, she glanced back to see the driver of the sedan. Recognizing him as Steven Vann, the man Lincoln first brought in from Limitless, her hands began to shake. Limitless was hunting her. It was certain now. She pulled down a side street and then another, watching in her mirror as she went. The trouble was, she didn't watch in front of her as readily. That's when the crash happened.

21

BOOYAH

Giving her the chance to get out of the convenience store lot and out of sight, Lincoln finished his conversation with Steven Vann. "I think you need to head back to Limitless and tell Victor or whoever that you failed to find Skye today."

Receiving a snarl in return, he quickly hopped into his truck and tapped the button on his steering wheel to call Ford.

"What's up?"

Pulling out of the lot, he decided to hang back so Vann didn't follow him. "Steven Vann was following Skye. She pulled into a convenience store and I blocked him. She's out there now without eyes on her."

"Shit. Which direction?"

"North on Second Street. I'm sure she's turning often so no way to know right now."

"On my way to your end of town."

Hearing the click, he immediately called Melissa's phone, knowing Skye was driving and not wanting to divert her attention. Her mother was clutching that phone like her life depended on it when Ford put them in the SUV. The pit in his stomach grew large and hot when the phone rang and rang and no one answered.

Seeing Steven Vann's sedan turn a couple of blocks back, he turned around in the road. Noticing Vann's quick turn down Remley Street, he dialed Dodge.

"Vann's moving down Remley Street, and I can't get the Sommerses on the phone."

"I'm close, I'll head there now."

"Any action at the Copper Cup?"

"Nothing."

"Okay, keep me posted. I'm going to have Jared start the tracking device."

A car stopped in front of him to make a left turn and another car parked on the right, leaving no way to go around him. Frustration burned in his gut. He tapped his Bluetooth button and said, "Call Jared Timm."

Finally able to move again, he turned down Remley Street and swore as he saw traffic up ahead. Deciding to make a U-turn and come in from a different direction, his breath seized in his chest when he saw Megan's SUV crumpled into a pile of metal and plastic two blocks up. Pulling as close as he could to the traffic jam, he jumped from his truck and ran to the SUV. People stood all around it on their phones. He gently pushed his way through the crowd, hoping they were all okay. When he finally got to the vehicle, the contents of his stomach nearly left his body.

The vehicle was empty.

His eyes whipped around to every person standing around. None of them were the Sommerses.

"Where are they? Where are the people who were in this vehicle?"

People mumbled that they didn't know and stepped away from the crazy man. A younger boy stood on the curb on the other side of the vehicle recording. Running over to him, he asked, "Did you see what happened here?"

"I was recording my grandpa over there on the porch, so I got it all on my phone."

"I need to see it, buddy."

"I need to finish recording. The cops will be here soon, and I want to get it all recorded so I can sell it to the news station in town."

"I'll pay you to show me now." Quickly pulling a twenty from his wallet, he shoved it at the boy who wrinkled his face up. Pulling another twenty, he handed it to the con artist posing as a boy and grabbed his phone. He looked into his photos, then videos, and what he saw made him throw up. Clutching the phone like a lifeline, he spit the vomit from his mouth, then started the video again.

Victor opened the driver's door right after the accident, grabbed Skye by her hair and yanked her from the car. Her face was bloody, and she seemed dazed. Two of his henchmen grabbed Melissa and Jeff, causing Jeff to cry out in pain as they roughly tossed him into the back of a van, one identical to the one that had been in front of the SUV. Skye was tossed into Victor's Mercedes with one of his minions in the backseat with her. The whole kidnapping took only a couple of minutes, as if it had been planned. The crowd of people grew as time passed.

Seeing the direction Victor had taken, he quickly emailed the video to himself, Ford, and Dodge. Giving the phone back to the kid, he asked, "How did you get away with recording them when they would have easily seen you?"

The kid shrugged. "I guess they wanted to be on video."

The sick thoughts that ran through his head made him dizzy. He ran back to his truck and turned around to catch up with the Mercedes.

Minutes later, his phone rang. "Yeah?"

"Where is she now?" Dodge's concern evident in his tone.

"I have no fucking idea, Dodge. I'm trying to follow the direction the Mercedes took, but by now, I don't have a chance. Where would that motherfucker take her?"

"Jared said you called him but you weren't on the line. I asked him to start the tracking device. Meet me back at Ford's."

"I can't." His voice broke, and he realized now that the shock was wearing off. His heart raced, and he was going to lose his shit in about two minutes. His hands shook, and he swallowed convulsively, trying to calm himself down. What he hadn't thrown up before threatened to tumble from his stomach now and he jabbed the button on the armrest to lower his window.

"Linc you can't help her driving around aimlessly. We have to calculate our next move and give Jared the time to locate her."

"That vicious bastard has her." His vision blurred and he angrily swiped at his eyes. "I was supposed to watch her. Protect her."

"Now we'll protect her in a different way. Go to the house. We'll have Jared on the line and we'll figure out where Victor's taken her."

The line went dead and his mind swirled with the worst thoughts.

His phone rang again and he jabbed the button on his steering wheel. "Tell me you've got something."

Ford responded, "Maybe. Come up the mountain. Now, Linc."

Taking a cleansing breath, he held it till his lungs burned. Only then releasing it. "Okay."

The call ended, and he headed his truck out of town and prayed with all he had that they had some helpful information.

Fifteen minutes later, he walked into Ford's house to the sounds of his partners making plans. Megan greeted him and wrapped her arms around his waist, whispering, "I'm so sorry."

He patted her back and gave her a squeeze. "Thanks, hon." Then he stepped past her and to the counter where his friends had maps laid out and highlighters at the ready.

Dodge nodded, his jaw tight. Ford's demeanor was similar. They didn't like losing one of their cases, and they sure as fuck didn't like this one. Skye had become so much more.

"Okay, Jared is on speaker right now and has emailed us information on property on the next mountain over owned by one of the Santarinos' companies. Skye's tracker is still going, but we don't have a lot of time, only three hours from the time it's activated."

Jared began explaining the area and how to access the private road and how to open the fence at the bottom of the drive. He always spoke with slow deliberation, something that never used to bother Lincoln, but right now he wanted this man to speed the fuck up.

Finally, he got to the part Lincoln was most interested in. "I can scramble the system once you get there, but it appears that they'll be alerted to the scramble. That will likely alert them to the fact that someone is coming and they no doubt are expecting that anyway, so your best bet is to give me an hour. I'll intermittently scramble their system and see how they handle it. If I keep doing it, they'll think their system is on the blink, and they'll either begin to ignore it, or they just might move the Sommerses. That would be best case scenario because we'd have a better shot at following. I suspect that would be their last resort though."

Keys could be heard clacking away as they waited for more information. "Got it. This will be better." He tapped a bit more then chuckled. "This is so good; I've been able to shut down their whole fucking network. This is fucking fantastic."

"What does that mean, their whole network? Computers only or cell phones too?" Lincoln asked.

"Let me try to scramble the cells."

Lincoln looked at his phone. It had been almost an hour since they'd taken Skye. Lord knows what they could be doing to her. "Wait! If you scramble the cells, will Skye's tracker work?"

"Booyah!" Jared cackled. "Cell phones scrambled. I'd bet you ten bucks they're packing up to leave as we speak. I'd say you have about fifteen minutes before you can get there, and it'll probably take them another few to get the Sommerses into vehicles. So, lay in wait at the bottom of the drive, amidst the heavy brush. I'll keep watching from here and keep their systems scrambled in case they're working on it. Lincoln, Skye's tracker is scrambled too. Can't do anything about that, but once they're on the move, I can re-engage the cells and the tracker will come back up."

His friends looked at him as if waiting for permission. He inhaled, nodded, and said, "Let's go," then headed to the door.

"Ford, put me on speaker in your truck," Jared said, still clicking away.

22

WE'RE GOING

Her first thought was she'd been drugged. Her second thought was, where were her parents? Her third thought was, where was Lincoln? She was so damned stupid. She just had to be involved in helping herself and look where she was now. She didn't know the actual location, but she sure as hell wasn't at home or in Lincoln's arms, and what she wouldn't give to be in his arms right now.

Her mind was fuzzy, and as she tried opening her eyes, they felt like lead. What she could tell right now was she was lying on a bed or mattress or something and the light was dim. Pulling her hands up to rub her eyes was futile; they were tied in front of her, bound at the wrists.

"Honey, are you all right? I was so worried."

"Mom?"

Her mom whispered, "Shh, yes, Daddy and I are here. They drugged you and your father. In his case, it's a blessing. They manhandled him and he was in a lot of pain, so at least he's resting easier now."

Whispering back, she asked, "Where are we?"

"I don't know. A room somewhere. I think we're up on a mountain. The drive here was winding upward, and the air is lighter like I felt at Ford and Megan's."

"I vaguely remember Victor pulling me from the SUV. I don't remember anything after that."

She tried her hands again, but she was too weak from whatever drug they'd injected her with.

"That van that pulled right in front of us—it was on purpose. Then an identical van pulled up, and your dad and I were tossed into the back. That's when they drugged him. He was howling in pain."

"Fucking bastards."

"Skye!" Her mother chastised her. Hearing her mom take a deep breath and let it out, she continued, "We need to be quiet, and if they come in here, you need to pretend to still be out or they might drug you again. I don't know what they're using, but it can't be good to have too much in your system."

"Where are you?"

"I'm across the room from you. I'm tied to your father."

Keys jangling in a lock halted her from saying more. She took her mother's advice and pretended to be out. She'd never been much of an actress, so she hoped like hell pretending to be asleep was easy. The door swung open, and everything was very quiet for a moment. "Who were you talking to in here?" a male voice commanded.

"I was praying. I'm sorry if I was loud." Her mom could be an actress; she sounded pious and contrite.

Hearing footsteps move closer to her, she focused on breathing even and deep as if she were still very much asleep. Rough hands gripped her chin and pulled her face toward him, but she managed to remain still. Bracing herself for a slap or other movement to see if she was faking, she waited, and it was scarier than anything else so far. She wasn't sure what would happen to her if they figured out she was faking. It could be far worse than she ever imagined. The hands left her chin and she heard the footsteps move across the room. The floor sounded like a wood floor or some kind of a laminate surface; his shoes made enough noise to be heard. Blessings came in many forms.

"He still out?"

"Yes. It's for the better since he's in so much pain all the time."

"Pray to yourself!" he snapped, then turned and left the room.

Once the door was closed and the key sounded in the lock, Skye allowed herself to let out a long breath.

Opening her eyes, she found she was a bit more lucid now, probably from the adrenaline flowing through her system. Again, blessings.

She could see a small window up high along the top of the wall across from her, letting in only a small amount of light, but it was enough that she could see her mom and dad lying on a bed across the room. Her mom waved to her, then held her hand bound to her father's in the air so she could see how they were tied together.

Lifting her head, she looked around the room. No furniture to speak of, just the two beds, one on either side of the room and one small table between them with nothing on it. Glancing at her wrists, she saw they were tied with a nylon rope. Her feet were not bound.

Straining to see if she could hear any sounds other than her father's even breathing, disappointment settled in her gut as she realized she couldn't tell a thing about where they were, how many people were out there, or anything else.

Not more than five minutes after that thought, she heard scrambling. A loud male voice barked out orders. "Find out what the fuck is going on with our network. Make sure the security system is working, and why the fuck can't I make a damned call?"

Victor. She'd know his voice anywhere.

Footfalls could be heard as people scrambled to do his bidding and fear clawed its way through her at the fact he was in an irritable mood. Victor on a good day wasn't pleasant. A pissed off Victor was deadly, as she so recently learned.

Sending up a silent prayer that Lincoln would find them soon, she lay as still as she could to not direct his anger toward her or her parents.

For the next few minutes, which seemed like hours, she could hear Victor bitching a tirade about their systems, their network, their cell phones, and what it all meant. Then words that chilled her reached her ears. "Should we just kill them?"

Oh God, no. Please don't let them be killed.

"No. Not yet. I need to know what her new boyfriend knows about what she saw and about my business, since you two stooges allowed yourselves to be seen committing murder. I don't know how many times I have to tell you to make sure no one is around when you do your jobs. I can't be everywhere with you. Right now, I have a mind to kill you two assholes for stupidity alone."

Oh. My. God. Her heart raced. The men she witnessed killing that poor agent were here. She wriggled her hands to see if she could loosen the rope, pleased that it seemed to work, if only a little. More bustling on the other side of the door alerted her to increased activity, and her breathing grew choppy. No way she'd be able to fake sleeping now.

Victor's voice yelled out, "Get them loaded in the van! We're going!"

23

SURPRISE

"Okay, they're on the move." Ford's voice sounded over the earbuds he'd plugged into his ears. Lincoln was sitting at the first side road at the bottom of the mountain Jared said Victor's gang was on. Since Victor surely knew his truck by now, he was on his Harley, dressed in full biker regalia, do-rag, mirrored shades, and leather jacket. His heart hammered. He couldn't fail this time. It could very well get Skye and her parents killed. Silently praying this plan would work and bolstering his own confidence, he listened as his friends called out locations. Ford, Dodge, and Rory Richards from Lynyrd Station PD were all set up at various locations on the mountain to watch for movement.

The rest of Lynyrd Station PD were on alert and at the ready, should any movement take place. A few of them were down the road in both directions with spikes set up to stop their vehicles. It would be a good time for the petty criminals in town to commit crimes, since all the local law enforcement was on this case at the moment. Grateful didn't come close to the feeling he had. He had some fantastic friends in places that mattered the most.

The first thing he'd do when he saw Skye again was hold her in his arms and vow to never fail her again. That is, if she'd even let him since she had every reason to hate him right now for letting her down.

Dodge's voice sounded in his ears. "I've got eyes on them. A van coming down the east side of the mountain."

Pressing the button on his earbud to engage the microphone, he asked, "Is Skye in it?"

"Can't tell. The trees have the road shaded here, and there aren't any windows in the back of the van."

Ford commented next. "How long before they reach the bottom of the road?"

"I'd say less than five," Dodge responded.

Craning his neck to see up the road for any movement, his eyes focused. Never one to let nerves take over when he needed to be coolheaded, he found himself fighting them now. Inhaling slowly, counting to five and then exhaling, he found a sense of calm. He had to do this and do it right.

"I've got eyes," Ford stated. "Bottom of the mountain road and turning toward you, Linc."

Pressing the button, he responded, "Roger. Has Jared unscrambled the house yet? Can he see where Skye is?"

Starting his bike, he put it in gear, made a U-turn, went down the road a few feet and U-turned again, hoping to make it to the end of the road just as the vehicles did, so it would look as though he was just a guy on a bike coming down the road. Luck on his side, he neared the intersection just as the van drove past.

Pulling out onto the road, he quickly pressed the

button on his buds and informed his colleagues, "I have eyes and following. Where's Skye?

Shifting into second gear, he stayed back slightly, fighting the urge to stay on top of them, until his partners were in place just up ahead.

A police cruiser, lights and sirens blaring, sped past him and the van before pulling into the lane in front of them. Not long after that, Ford's truck came up behind him, passed and did the same. Dodge wasn't far behind but stayed just behind Lincoln, offering backup at the rear. Now that they were all in place, shit could happen.

Rory sounded first. "Get ready. Roadblock in two tenths of a mile."

His ear buds cracked. "Linc, Skye isn't in the van. Victor must be taking her in a separate vehicle, and Jared is tracking them on the other side of the mountain."

"Shit!" he spat out, whipped his bike around in the road, and raced down the county road to the intersecting road that would take him to the other side.

"Keep me posted. I don't have eyes over here," he yelled over the wind into his microphone.

Ford responded a moment later. "Head to McKinnley Road and take a right. They still aren't at the bottom of the mountain."

Okay, he knew where McKinnley was. He took a perp down that road his first week in town. Twisting the throttle, he gunned his bike, blowing past mailboxes and country lanes. Nearing McKinnley, he slowed to make the turn but quickly changed course when he saw Victor's Mercedes nearing the county road he was traveling on from the mountain road. He didn't want to be in front of Victor and certainly didn't want to make any evasive moves to alert Victor that he was more than a biker out for a ride. Luck was on his side when Victor pulled out in front of him. He swerved to the side of the road but didn't have to slow down much more because Victor stepped on the gas.

His heart hammered when a gorgeous blonde head lifted from the backseat and looked back at him. The white gag in her mouth raised his blood pressure to near boiling and the evil thoughts that raged through his brain scared him. Never had he felt such an overpowering urge to protect and possess.

Dodge's voice sounded in his ear. "We've got the Sommerses—senior Sommerses—that is."

Okay, so that was good news. Now he just had to keep his eye on Skye. She looked back again, and rubbing the tension from his neck and tilting his head from side to side, hoping to let her know it was him. Recognition was unlikely right now the way he was dressed.

Victor reached back and grabbed her hair in one hand as his car swerved. He saw her head snap back then fall back to the seat. His breath held, afraid Victor would lose control of the car and kill them both. He wanted the plea-sure of taking a piece or two of Victor first.

Ford's truck raced up behind him, then passed him, but not before Ford formed a circle with his hand, signaling that he'd pull in front of Victor, so don't get too close.

Backing off just enough to allow Ford the room he needed, his friend pulled up alongside the Mercedes, then tapped the side of the car with his truck. Victor struggled with the car a bit and Lincoln's lungs burned as he held his breath. Tapping the car once again, it skidded and swerved but began to slow just enough that he had to lower his speed behind them.

Ford tapped again and Skye's head lifted once more, looked in his direction, and nodded once. She recognized him. Relief.

Ford tapped once again, and at the same time, Skye reached forward and pulled Victor's head back, causing him to lose control of the car. The car lost speed and Ford's truck bumped against the car which turned them slightly to the ditch alongside the road. Gravel began flying at him from the back tires, but he hunkered down and stayed with the slowing vehicle.

The Mercedes hit the ditch, lurched up and back down, and came to a grinding halt. He was off his bike in a matter of seconds and running to the car. Flinging open the backdoor, he saw that Skye's hands were tied in front of her, but she'd wrapped them around Victor's neck, braced her knees on the back of the seat and was strangling him. Victor had stopped all movement by the time he got to them.

"Skye, honey, you can let him go. I've got you."

Her wild eyes stared at him but she didn't seem to comprehend what he'd said. Glancing at her hands, he saw they had turned purple from the strain and he worried she'd do permanent damage to herself.

"Princess, let go, baby. I've got you."

Reaching forward, he placed his hand over one of hers, and the connection seemed to register in her eyes. Her bottom lip quivered, and he saw the tears begin to form. "I've got you, okay?"

He pulled her hands forward slightly, just enough to release the pressure and allow herself to pull them over Victor's head.

The driver's door whipped open and Ford reached in, grasping Victor's hands to keep him from harming anyone in retaliation. Ford's eyes met his as he disengaged Skye's hands from around Victor's neck. Ford shook his head slowly, telling him they'd have no more issues with Victor Santarino.

Reaching into the backseat of the car, he slid his hand under her legs and then behind her to pull her out. The blood had dried on her face, and he could see bruises forming. Her clothes were bloody, and her hair had been pulled and tugged and used as a handle Lord only knew how many times today. But still, underneath all of that, there was the princess he first saw standing in her Jimmy Choos and expensive suit, looking more regal than any woman he'd ever met.

Setting her on the tailgate of Ford's truck, he pulled his knife from his back pocket. His eyes sought hers. "I'm only cutting the rope off your wrists, princess. Okay?"

Her head bobbed once, and he made quick work of cutting the rope away, being as careful as he'd ever been. Once her hands were free, he began to massage her fingers and palms, bringing blood flow to them and examining her for injuries. Removing her gag, he placed a light kiss to her injured lips and continued to care for her hands.

The faint wail of sirens sounded, and for the first time, she mumbled, "My parents."

"We've got them. I'll take you to the hospital to get checked out and then you can see them."

"They're alive?"

He glanced at Ford, who nodded. "Yes, princess, they're alive."

24

NOW SHE WAS A MURDERER

"One more question, and I'll let you rest, Ms. Sommers. Tell me what your relationship to the Santarino family is. I've seen many pictures of you with Mangus Santarino at various events. I also know he's married. Tell me where you fit in."

"I don't fit in anywhere. I work for Limitless and those pictures are not what they seem. I've shown Lincoln the proof of that." She looked to Lincoln, hoping he'd confirm that fact.

"She's right. I did see the proof that those pictures had been doctored or clipped to look like they were something they were not. I can get you the proof to clear your file."

The Homicide Detective wrote something down on a notepad, and she fidgeted with the sheet on the hospital bed.

"Why would someone doctor photos to look like an affair or relationship was going on?"

"I thought you only had one more question." Biting her lip, she realized that sounded a bit bitchy, but today had been a shitty day.

Lincoln leaned forward from the chair he sat in alongside her bed and took her hand in his. "I have a theory, if you want to hear it."

Her eyes traveled to his and held. The detective stopped writing, looked at Lincoln, and slightly nodded.

"I think it was Victor trying to drive Mangus out of the company, or at the very least, create issues for him. Victor is the younger of the Santorino brothers. When Giovanni, their father, dies, Mangus is slated to run the company. He wants to back out of the arms smuggling and stick with art and jewelry. Probably not totally legit, but certainly not as dangerous as the arms smuggling. I have a recording of the brothers arguing about this very issue not more than a year and a half ago. I can't tell you how I came across the recording, but you can listen to it if you like. I think by casting Mangus as an adulterer, his wife would leave him, his personal life would crumble and much of their business holdings would need to be separated since Mangus's wife owns many of their real estate holdings in her name. It would tie Mangus up to deal with all of that while Victor could continue to move ahead with his money-making ventures in the arms dealing."

The officer stared for a long while, saying nothing. Turning her head to look at Lincoln, she saw his jaw clenched and his forehead furrowed.

He looked up at her and slightly shrugged. "I'm sorry, princess. It seems you've been used at every turn through all of this, but I honestly believe that's what was going on with the pictures."

"I'll head back to the police station now." He handed them each his business card. "Lincoln, send me the information you have on the Santarinos and the pictures so we can wrap up our file. Ms. Sommers, at this time, I feel confident that the prosecutor's office will agree that this case should be closed and determined self-defense. No charges should be forthcoming. If you think of anything else we need to know, give me a call."

She stared at his card for a long time, gathering her thoughts as the relief fully washed over her. Blinking furiously in hopes it would stem the tears from flowing. Because Lord have mercy, she'd been crying on and off for the past three hours. The doctor said it was the trauma, drugs coming out of her system, and hormones. Admitting that was undoubtedly part of it, she'd also never killed a man before and never dreamed she ever would, so now, she was a murderer. No better than Victor himself.

"You're not a murderer, princess. Stop letting your thoughts go there."

"How do you know what I'm thinking?" Looking into those steel gray eyes, she had to admit, she felt calmer. Safer. His big presence in her room for the past couple of hours helped her more than she had a right to be helped.

"I can tell by the look on your face."

Perching his fabulous ass on the edge of her bed, he faced her, took the lotion from her bedside tray, squirted a healthy amount into his large hands and rubbed them together. Gently pulling her hands toward him, he smoothed the lotion over her red, swollen, and bruised wrist and fingers. Her eyes were glued to the movement of his hands as they slowly massaged hers. His deep sexy voice then began soothing her further.

"These hands right here care for parents who love you. Animals that need you and fly over the keys on your computer faster than any I've ever seen. Last night, they touched me, held me, caressed me and made me feel like the man I want to be but never felt I was. Finally, these hands have saved countless people from unspeakable fates at the hands of Victor Santarino."

Repeating the motions on her other hand, he never slowed his movements, and continued wooing her with his words.

"I want these hands to hold mine in times of happiness, times of hardship, and times of sadness. I want these hands to care for me and my pup."

He kissed each finger, his eyes never leaving hers. "I love you, Skye."

Her heartbeat sped up and she probably just imagined that he said he loved her, so she took the offensive. "You can't love me. We've only known each other for a few days."

"Doesn't matter. I fell in love with you the second I laid eyes on you. I figured it out when you'd been taken from me. I knew it completely when I saw you fight to stay alive."

A sigh from the other side of the room had her turning her head to see her mom entering the room, tears in her eyes, her hands held over her heart as if it would burst from her chest.

"You have to stop doing that. You're going to give him a big head."

Melissa sniffed, straightened her posture, squared her shoulders, and replied, "There isn't a woman alive who wouldn't want to hear those words from a man like Lincoln." Moving to her bed, her mom kissed her temple, then stood back to look at her. Lincoln never stopped massaging lotion into her raw wrists. "Detective Jacobs told me they didn't think charges would be forthcoming. That's just fantastic news."

"It is fantastic. How's Daddy?" Her mind struggled

with paying attention to Lincoln and speaking with her mom.

"He's doing well." Addressing Lincoln, she said, "I'm so grateful you found that Acepromazine in Victor's car. They've been able to bring him around and he's going to be just fine, the doctor said. Also, you were right about his medications, too. Megan is in there right now talking to the doctors with her list of his medications to see if they can figure out where everything went wrong."

Lincoln looked up from his busy work. "I'm glad I found it, too. I'd have a hard time forgiving myself if I hadn't been able to help all of you. I promised to keep you safe. I like keeping my promises." Lifting Skye's right hand, he kissed the back of it, and she shot her mother a scathing look, knowing the sigh was coming.

Pinching her lips together, her mom instead announced, "I'll be going back to your father's room. I'll pop back in later." Turning quickly, she left the room.

Catching his steely gaze with hers, she ran the backs of her fingers down his cheek and jaw, enjoying the stubble that had formed over the past several hours. "I love you, too, Lincoln. It's the strangest thing, but I can't help it. You're everything I ever wanted and so much more. And I also owe you a big thank you for saving my family and me."

His head slowly began moving toward hers, and when impatience got the better of her, she leaned up, let out a breath at the shot of pain that lanced through her chest, but met his lips halfway regardless.

The softness in his kiss was the best medicine for her now. For the first time since she'd seen him last, she felt as if life was going to be just fine. Nope, probably pretty frickin' fantastic, as long as Lincoln was with her.

The door to her room opened, and Ford popped his head in. "I have a couple of visitors, if you don't mind."

She nodded, eager to see who was here and thrilled when Megan, Abe, and Dodge entered the room. Megan let Abe off his leash and he ran first to Lincoln for snuggles and affection, then his front paws jumped up on the bed and he laid his head on her lap.

"Aww, you are such a sweet boy, Abe," she crooned to him as she petted his head.

Megan softly asked, "How are you, Skye?" Her eyes focused on the red abrasions on her wrists and then the bruises on her face, which she hadn't inspected yet, but just from Megan's reaction, she assumed they weren't very attractive.

"I'm fine, Megan. No broken bones, just bruises and abrasions." She held up her hands as if to clarify. "I'll get to go home in a little while. They're just making sure the drug is out of my system. Or mostly, anyway."

Dodge moved forward and looked her in the eye. She hadn't had much interaction with Dodge during all of this, but Linc had told her how hard he worked to help with her and her family. His eyes then landed on her wrists and his lips turned down into a frown.

"It's okay Dodge, they'll heal."

"Yeah." His voice was unusually soft. He was normally the brash one in the group. "I'm sorry anyway, we probably should have had a better plan."

Shaking her head, she fought those damnable tears again. "That's what we all get for working with amateurs." She reached for his hand and squeezed his fingers. "I won't make that mistake again. I don't know how you guys do this stuff on a regular basis, but my one and only time is more than enough for me."

Megan rested her hand on the top of her belly and patted Abe's head. "I'm so glad Lincoln had that tracker on you."

Tracker? Her spine stiffened as she turned her gaze to meet Lincoln's. "Tracker?"

Abe's head lifted from her lap and he whined. Lincoln seemed wary as he answered her. "When I pulled you to me by the front pockets of your jeans, I dropped a tracker in your pocket. Not because I didn't trust you to do what needed to be done, but there were so many variables, and I needed to know that I could find you if the worst happened." He captured her hand in his. "And it did. I'm not sorry."

He had a point. It would have been nice to know there'd been a contingency plan so maybe she wouldn't have been so damned scared, but in the end, it had all worked out.

The door opened and a doctor walked in the room. Walking around her guests, his eyes glanced at Abe, who snarled slightly, but Lincoln settled him by saying, "*Fruend.*"

Abe studied Lincoln's face for a moment, then glanced at the doctor who seemed reluctant to come any closer. Lincoln clicked his tongue a couple of times and Abe heeled at his side, allowing the doctor enough space to tend to her. He was a great dog.

"My name is Dr. Josten, and I'm here to make sure you're well enough to go home." He shined his light in her eyes, examined her wrists, looked at the abrasions on her head, and the bruises on her chest from the airbag hitting her. "I can release you if you have someone staying with you overnight. Just as a precaution."

Lincoln spoke before she could get the words out. "I'll be with her."

"Fantastic. Then I'll have the nurse get your release papers ready to go."

Ford spoke for the first time since entering the room. "Linc, I brought my Mustang to town and Megan drove my truck. I'll leave the truck here for you." Handing Linc the keys, Ford nodded to him, "Have you got Abe? Megan has a doctor appointment in a few minutes. That's the other reason we're here."

"Yeah, thanks for bringing him to town, I've got him."

Dodge leaned forward and kissed the top of her head, shook hands with Lincoln and patted Abe's head. "I'll take off too. See you in a day or so."

The room quieted as her guests left but Lincoln was quick to break the silence. "I want you to stay at my place, Skye. Until we know how far Victor's tentacles reach and whether danger has passed, I'd like you to stay with me."

25

—————

MY WATER BROKE

"Well, I just can't believe that Brian Lochlain's son, Brian, Jr., would try to harm us in any way. We've known that kid since he was born." Melissa swiped her palms down her thighs, the worry line between her brows deepened. "I never thought of him as a troubled teen."

"It seems more like he was nosy than troubled." Dodge answered. "The PD said he heard about the murder and he knew that Jeff had been injured, so he was poking around. More of an opportune criminal if anything. He also won't admit to being there with someone else. The investigator thinks he hit his head on the shovel when he tried to dive under the shrubbery to hide from your vehicles."

This family had been put through the wringer of late. Looking around the table, Lincoln saw his friends, who truthfully, were more like family to him. Megan and Skye brought more food to the table, and he frowned slightly as his eyes landed on the fading marks on her wrists. Fucking Victor.

Jeff announced, "I'd like to say grace, please."

Everyone folded their hands and bowed their heads, and he listened to every word. They all said, "Amen," then began digging into the nice spread of food Megan, Skye, and Melissa had made for them all.

"So, when do you think we'll be able to go home?" Jeff asked before taking a big bite of mashed potatoes.

This was a good topic of conversation, so he was happy to finally bring them some good news.

Setting his fork down, he took Skye's hand and gave it a slight squeeze. "Tomorrow. Lynyrd Station PD has rounded up Victor's henchmen. They all sang like birds as soon as Vann, Rodriquez, and Russo were captured—each of them wanting a plea deal more than the others. Rodriquez and Russo were the ones who killed Agent Masters, so there's no plea deal for them."

Skye twisted to look at him. "That's wonderful." Then looking at Megan, she quickly added, "Not that your hospitality is bad. Goodness, you've taken better care of my parents than I could ever hope, but it's good to get back to our regular routine again."

"Well, honey, about that." Melissa set her fork down and looked at Jeff. He nodded, so she continued, "We're selling the ranch and moving to River's Edge to be closer to Devin and the grandkids. Daddy's better now that he isn't on all those meds anymore, but we can't work the farm like we should and it would take too much to bring it back to what it was. Brian Lochlain is buying it from us, and at a fantastic price, I might add, probably because he feels bad about his son trying to steal from us. But anyway, he's been taking care of the few animals we have there and he's ready to sign papers as soon as we can move our belongings out of the house."

Lincoln watched Skye process this news, swallow a few times and stare at her mother as if she'd spoken in tongues. Jeff spoke up then, "Skye, honey, it's for the best. We're making lemonade out of lemons. We see our situation for what it is, and to be honest, I feel a huge relief after making this decision."

Melissa took her daughter's other hand in hers and continued, "Honey, you can't keep working two jobs and build a life with Lincoln. It's too much and we shouldn't have relied on you for as long as we have. Devin has been angry with us about leaning so heavily on you and so have Logan and Savannah. They've been pressing us to do something for such a long time. It's only forty-five minutes away."

Skye nodded, then whispered, "Of course, "She cleared her throat, "I don't have two jobs anymore. Limitless is closed, and now I don't have the farm either." She shook her head, and he watched her process everything, and for the life of him, he didn't know what to do to help her, other than continue to hold her hand as long as she wanted him to. Melissa leaned over and kissed Skye on the temple and softly said, "It's perfect, then. You have time to decide what you want to do. We'll have enough money from the farm to replenish your savings and a little more to give you that time."

Megan dropped her fork and gasped. All eyes turned to her. "My water broke!"

Everyone stood, except Dodge who continued eating the last bits on his plate.

Lincoln looked at Ford for guidance because honest to God, he didn't know what to do now. "Okay, Linc, can you get my truck turned around and ready to drive down to town? Skye and Melissa, I'm sorry but can you clean up once you're finished eating? Dodge?" He looked at his other friend and grinned. "I'm going to be a father again. You're going to need to help Linc with the business for a few days."

Dodge's brows furrowed. "I'm used to being out on the road catching scum. I don't do paperwork and make phone calls, Ford."

"I can. That would be perfect. Let me help you, please." Skye's eyes were bright, her lips formed the perfect smile, and her cheeks flushed with color.

Megan found her voice. "Skye, you'd be perfect at the office work. It's mostly organized and the bills I was going to work on tomorrow are in the red folder on the desk. Password is written on the inside of it."

"I won't let you down."

Ford clapped his hands. "Chop, chop folks, we've got to get to the hospital."

Brusquely walking to Ford's truck, he couldn't help but smile. Things were beginning to shape up. Now he just had to figure out a way to keep Skye at his place because he liked having her there.

26

I'LL GET IT

Handing Lincoln a beer, she sat in the deck chair next to his, clinked her beer bottle to his and took a swig. The river was flowing gently, the sun an hour or so from setting and the temperature mild. A perfect night to sit and relax. The past three weeks had been a little bit of hell mixed with a lot of happy. This being the happy.

"Is this a perfect evening for you? A good evening for you? Or just a tolerable evening for you, Skye?"

Turning her head, her brows furrowed as she looked at him. "What a weird question. It's a perfect evening. Why would you ask it in that way?"

"I wondered if a perfect evening for you would be champagne and caviar on a yacht somewhere."

She sat back as if pushed. "Champagne and caviar on a yacht sounds like something movie stars or the very rich enjoy. I've never lived that life, and it never comes to mind that I'm missing it, to be honest." Abe bounded from the river, shook his coat and the tiny sparkles as the sun hit the flying water caught her attention. Then it hit her.

Sitting forward and twisting to look into Lincoln's eyes, she asked, "Are you asking because of my Jimmy Choos? You commented on them once before. Do you think I'm looking for caviar and champagne and a man who can provide that for me?"

He took a long pull from his beer, then let out a breath. "I've been down that road, Skye. Jenny, my ex, wanted everything money could buy. Sitting in a wooden chair on a deck looking at the river and my dog while drinking a beer wasn't something she'd ever do."

She laughed then, probably because she'd been nervous about his answer. "To be honest with you Linc, my ex and your ex should get together, because they sound like two peas in a pod."

She drank from her bottle, watched Abe jump into the water and quickly pop out with a stick in his mouth and laughed again. "This is perfect."

Before her mind could think another thought, she was scooped from her chair and carried into the house. Looking into Lincoln's face, she saw determination and happiness. His features were relaxed more than she'd ever seen him; his full lips formed a small smile. His eyes trained on the path he was taking, which she knew was straight to the bedroom, but he knew she was watching him. The cords in his neck relaxed a bit and her hand, which had flown over his neck when she was picked up, splayed over his firm, defined shoulders, enjoying the movement of them as he walked. Dang, she was lucky.

"Look all you want, princess. I'll be doing the same thing to you in about two more minutes."

That sent a shiver down her spine and a tingle that rested between her legs. Damn.

He released her feet but they didn't touch the floor.

His arm expertly held her body to his, chest to chest, her face just an inch lower than his. Curling her other arm around his shoulder, she kissed his lips, a slight moan escaping her throat when his tongue entered her mouth and gently swiped along her tongue. He was good at kissing.

Nipping lightly at her lips a couple of times, he let her slide slowly down his body. There was no mistaking his intent as it pushed into her lower belly. Looking into his eyes, a soft smile spread her lips, and she grew bold.

"What do you want, Linc?" She unbuttoned his jeans, slowly lowered his zipper, never looking away from his stormy eyes. "You want my lips on you down here?"

Emphasizing where "down here" was, she cupped his cock through the denim he wore. His nostrils flared slightly and his breathing hitched a bit.

"I want you to say it first, princess. Tell me what that means."

Oh, so that's how he was going to play it. She'd bet his ex-wife never gave him head. She was too worried about messing up her five-hundred-dollar hair style or her perfect manicure. She'd give him a dirty girl. It would be fun.

"Do you want me to suck your cock, Lincoln? Swirl my tongue around the top of your hard dick, and lick the pre-cum from its head?"

Tucking her thumbs into the sides of his jeans, she tugged them down and slowly went down on her knees in front of him as she dragged his jeans and shorts with her.

His rigid cock bobbed slightly before her, and wasting no time, she covered him with her mouth. Cupping his balls with one hand, she wrapped her other hand around the base of his cock and slowly pumped him in time with her mouth. His size was impressive and wetness raced to her pussy as she remembered how he felt sliding inside of her. Clinching her thighs together, she hoped it wasn't enough to trickle down her thighs.

Pulling him from her mouth, she ran her tongue along the underside of his cock, flicking it back and forth until the course hairs tickled her nose. Deciding to give him the best she could give, her tongue swathed a wet trail from the base of his cock all the way past his balls. She knew that was the perfect move when they drew up into his sac. Score one for Skye.

His hands dug into her hair, his fingers massaging her scalp as his hips began rocking. The groan that escaped his throat was guttural and pure. She smiled, and the thrill that ran through her was intoxicating. Giving this man pure pleasure was heady and exciting.

Her mouth wrapped around his cock once more, making him grunt and exhale loudly. Bobbing her head faster, her hand keeping time with her mouth, she knew he was close. Bringing her mouth down on him as far as she could, she moaned, and the vibration must have sent a chill through him because she'd never heard a sound like the one he made, so she did it again. This caused him to hiss and pull her head back from him. Stiffening her neck, she sucked him in and held.

"Skye, I won't last ..."

Reaching back, she placed her hand over his in her hair and squeezed before going back to cup his balls once more. Then she felt the warm spurt to the back of her throat and quickly swallowed as he continued to release himself in her mouth. He stood stock still for a moment as she gently sucked one last time and let him gently fall from her lips.

Wiping the sides of her mouth, she looked up at him and smiled at the look he gave her. Awe, that's what it was. He was awed. Perfect.

A phone ringing in the distance caught her attention first. Pulling back, she stood, looked into his glazed eyes, then said, "I'll get it. Maybe Megan had the baby."

27

PROBABLY THE BEST THING HE COULD HAVE HEARD

It took his brain a moment to realize Skye had left the room. Dazed and confused wasn't how he planned that to shake out. Pulling his pants up, he zipped his jeans as he walked down the hall to Skye and his fucking phone.

The smile on her gorgeous face as she handed him his phone was beguiling. This woman was something else.

"It's Ford." She giggled.

He took his phone in one hand and her hand in the other and led them to the sofa. Sitting down, pulling her close to him and tapping the speaker icon, he addressed his friend. "Are you calling with news?"

"Yes, we have a dark-haired, light-eyed baby girl."

"What does that mean, light-eyed?"

His friend chuckled. "They seem blue now, but I've been told all babies' eyes are blue unless they're brown and they just might change later. So, I'm hoping she has Meg's eyes."

Skye was the first to giggle and say, "Congratulations

to both of you and happy birthday to ... Oh, what did you name her?"

She looked into his eyes, the sparkle in hers breathtaking. Happiness was written all over her face and it hit him, since he'd met her, this was the first time she'd been relaxed and happy and just herself. He loved this Skye even more than the other one, the one in trouble and on the run.

"We named her Shelby in keeping with the car names, since I already have Falcon, and Ann for a middle name which was Megan's grandmother's middle name."

Skye giggled again and he chuckled. "Congratulations, my friend. We couldn't be happier for the two of you."

"Thanks. Gotta go. I have a few more calls to make. Oh, and not to throw in business, but Rory has details on GHOST. In the morning, give him a call. It's an interesting outfit, and I'm wondering if we may want to try and touch base with them. We could maybe do some of their lower level type stuff. It's a badass organization by the sounds of it."

Now his curiosity was piqued. "Take care." He hit the end call icon and looked at his princess. "Are you hungry or thirsty? And, I didn't forget that I still owe you an orgasm. I promise to make it up to you."

Leaning up on her knees, she kissed his lips softly then leaned back. "Why don't I make us something to eat? You'll want to call Rory right away so you can do that while I cook."

"It can wait till morning, princess."

She stood and walked around the sofa and laughed again. "I can tell and know you well enough by now to know it'll be on your mind until you call him. And when you pay me back later, I only want that on your mind."

"Well, fuck me," he muttered, then quickly dialed Rory despite the fact that it was six thirty in the evening.

The phone rang once, and Rory's all-business voice sounded. "I'll bet you're already calling about GHOST."

"You know it. Tell me what you've got."

Rory laughed then began. "GHOST Stands for Government Hidden Ops Specialty Team. They are a secret organization comprised of former military personnel. Often hired by our government to perform tasks the government has no stomach for or can't get the authority to do. They are also hired by others to accomplish tasks for mostly very wealthy individuals. They come at a great expense and their training is stellar. Agent Jake Masters, who Victor had killed, was one of their agents, and they want blood. I can't get the information as to who hired them to infiltrate the Santarinos, but rumor has it it's someone they screwed in an arms deal."

"Holy fuck. With Victor gone, are they still going after Mangus?"

"It appears so. And, my informant tells me they already have someone in place here in Lynyrd Station. We're watching the situation closely."

"Do you have any idea of some of the missions they've accomplished?"

"No. It's all very secretive, and my understanding is that if one of them is caught by any authority, the government will deny any knowledge or working relationship with them, so they're very careful. Underground, even."

A cold beer tapped his shoulder and he looked back to see Skye smiling at him, holding a beer over his shoulder then winking before walking away. Sexy.

"Thanks, Rory. Gotta run."

Ending the call, he followed Skye to the kitchen where

delicious smells were floating in the air and singing a siren's song to him.

He walked up behind her, wrapped his arms around her waist and pulled her back from the counter where she was mixing up a pasta salad. He was already hard when her ass hit his cock, and the thought of tasting her was more important than any food available. He heard her sigh and he almost teased her that she sounded like her mother. Silly woman sighed around him all the time. But, he wasn't a stupid man, so he held his tongue.

His hands slid up under the T-shirt she wore, under her bra and covered her glorious breasts. Breasts he'd thought about day and night since the moment he met her, if he were an honest man. Her head rested against his shoulder and her breathing grew choppy. She was his in this moment, and that was heavenly. The little denim cut-off shorts she wore were sexy beyond belief, but he wanted them gone. His lips kissed the shell of her ear, then whispered, "Take your shorts off, princess."

Her hands complied with his demand and he smiled when he heard the zipper lower. His bare feet felt her shorts drop on top of them, and one of his hands lowered to find her panties still in place. "These too, sweetheart."

Her nipples puckered and he chuckled in her ear. "You like that? You're gonna really like what I have in mind."

He felt the goose bumps form on her arms as his hand found her clit. She struggled only slightly to lower her panties and her bare ass hit his cock. Even through his jeans, he could feel the difference, and his cock thickened immediately. Turning her around, he tucked his hands under her arms, lifted her onto the counter and spread her knees apart, focusing his attention on the beautiful glistening pussy in his sights. Scooting her to the edge of the counter, he bent and ran his tongue along her seam and was rewarded with a moan from deep in her chest.

His forefinger slid into her easily as his tongue flicked over her clit and teased. Pumping his finger in and slowly out, he enjoyed the little sounds she made, all of them sensual and happy. Sucking her clit into his mouth and flicking his tongue over it while keeping the pressure earned him a loud moan and even his name from her lips. That sounded like heaven.

When his cock throbbed, he began kissing his way up her body, pushing her T-shirt up. Along the way, he enjoyed the ripples of her tummy as her muscles clenched and relaxed. Reaching behind her, he unsnapped her bra and enjoyed the feel of her full breasts as they fell from their confines. Sucking one into his mouth quickly earned him another great moan.

Giving attention to first one breast then the other, he stood back just a moment, pulled his finger from her and chuckled when her glazed eyes landed on his. "I'll replace it soon, princess."

Making quick work of his pants and feeling grateful he was commando, his aching cock fell easily into his hand. He expertly rolled on a condom, then guided himself to that sweet pussy before him. Swirling the broad head around her tender tissues, he saw her eyes watching his movements. "Doesn't that look good, princess? You and me together. Watch as I disappear inside of you."

Positioning the firm broad head at her entrance, he was conflicted between watching her face or watching as his body slide into hers. Her face won as he wanted to see her expression and he wasn't disappointed. Her plump lips formed an O and her attention was fully on their bodies. She clenched her Kegel muscles and it was his turn to moan. Her body felt so fucking good.

Holding on to her backside as much as he could, he pulled her to the edge of the counter as far as he could for easy access. Pushing up into her, he could hear her breathing huff out in puffs, so he pushed himself into her harder. A little cry of pleasure tumbled from her lips as her arms wrapped around his shoulders. "Princess, use your fingers on your clit."

Leaning back again, she braced herself with one arm and circled her clit with her fingers. Then the little vixen lowered her finger so it ran along his cock as he pulled out of her and pushed back in. That was an interesting sensation. The groan he emitted earned him a smile and their eyes locked. Their rhythm increased, and it felt amazing.

"Linc, I'm close."

That was his cue. He wrapped his arms tightly around her and pulled her off the counter, leaning on his arms for support and began pumping into her wildly. The exertion formed a sheen on his chest and back, her legs tightening around his waist. Tilting her pelvis up as he pushed in created a sensation that threatened to make him explode before she did. Just in the nick of time, she cried out as her orgasm rolled over her, and he let himself go.

Huffing out as his orgasm seemed to roll on and on, he laid his head on her shoulder and was rewarded with her arms tightening around his shoulders and her warm breath in his ear. "That was hot, Linc. I've never done anything like that before."

Probably the best thing he could have heard.

"From now on, though, let's ditch the condoms."

No, that was the best thing he could have heard.

28

THAT'S HOW I FEEL TOO

Four days later, Skye sat at a desk in Lincoln's office. One they had purchased for her that matched his desk. They butt them up so when she wanted to she could stare at him deep in thought, because honestly, who wouldn't want to just sit and stare at him all day like she was doing now. A little sigh escaped her lips and he looked up at her, his brows in the air.

"Don't make me say it, princess."

She shook her head and she giggled. "Sorry." He'd told her once before she sounded like her mother, and she couldn't deny that she did. In the beginning she'd been so focused on not getting in trouble at work that she didn't really allow herself to see his true beauty. Now that she did, it was breathtaking. He was breathtaking.

He closed the lid on his laptop, opened the top drawer of his desk, pulled something from it and closed it. "Princess, it's time we talked."

Her brows lifted and she sat straighter in her chair. "Okay." That didn't sound good.

"The first time I met you and we talked, we were sitting

just like this. Well, almost. You were seated behind your desk and I was staring at you as your fingers flew over your keyboard, locating Steven Vann within Limitless. I remember thinking you were such a vision, a princess ruling a kingdom but doing it with grace and dignity. Little did we know then what things really were. But I also remember thinking I'd love to know more about you. And I still want that. We've gotten to know each other as we've lived together for a few weeks now, but it isn't permanent."

He stood and walked to the side of her desk, his eyes never left hers. Her heartbeat raced and her throat dried out. Questions flew through her mind at warp speed, but a coherent thought wouldn't present itself. He turned her chair so she faced him and she couldn't look away.

"I'd like to make this arrangement permanent. Us working together, living together, getting to know each other. I have a feeling for the rest of my life, I'll keep learning new things about you, and I'll find each one of them fascinating."

He kneeled down on one knee in front of her, the tiny object in his hand held before her. A gorgeous ring of platinum and diamonds. Stunning, sparkling and a representation of something she'd longed for once again. Marriage, a family, stability.

"Will you marry me, Skye Sommers of Sommers' Dreams? Will you be Skye Winter of Winter Valley?"

Staring into his eyes, she wanted this moment imprinted on her mind forever. For the first time in her life, even though she'd been married before, this one was the one. This man before her was the man she'd been looking for.

Feelings bubbled up inside of her: happiness, excitement, and so much love. "Yes. My God, yes."

Placing her hands on either side of his head, she held him and kissed his lips. The instant her lips touched his, tears fell from her eyes, tracked down her cheeks and fell onto them. She didn't care; they were tears of happiness.

He pulled back and swiped the tears from her cheeks with his thumb, kissed her nose, and placed the ring on her finger. Stunning was the only word she could think of to describe it. He'd chosen perfectly. As if he knew what was going on, Abe bounded into the room and licked her face, then flopped down on the floor and onto his back so she could scratch his belly. "That's how I feel about you, too, princess. I love you."

Giggling, she finally felt she could talk without ugly crying. "I love you, too." Abe's tail thumped and they both laughed.

29

YOU CAN WEAR THE SHOES

Skye wandered among the tuxedos, suits, ties of all styles, and vests of many colors. This store smelled like new clothing and starch. The clerk stood behind the counter, taping something into the computer and glancing at her every now and then.

Pulling her phone from her purse, she glanced first at the time, then to see if she had any missed messages. Where in the hell was Lincoln? For that matter, where were all of the guys? Ford and Dodge, too. She'd give them a few more minutes before she called him.

Turning toward the ties, she looked them over and mentally hoped he'd be open to wearing the gray and black ascot tie. They hadn't talked about any of these details they'd been so busy lately. But he'd look like her Prince Charming in a tux and ascot. Of course, he always looked that way.

They'd neglected many details, such as tux selection and fitting, until this week, the week of their wedding, moving her parents to Rivers Edge which was closer to her brother. That was a monumental task. Moving forty plus years worth of household items and treasures from their home had lent itself to many arguments, hurt feelings, and an incredible amount of time. Never in her life had the thought occurred to her that she'd make her mother cry by pointing out that some of the things they'd collected in their married life weren't important to her and her siblings. To them, it was just stuff. Their condo was much smaller, which oddly, made both of her parents quite happy. But the purging of accumulated mementos was heartbreaking. People amass so much stuff! She'd made a note to herself, don't collect so much stuff.

At the same time, she had to move out of her apartment, which luckily wasn't nearly the undertaking of her parents' home, but she and Lincoln still had made decisions as to what furniture they'd keep and what they'd get rid of; in the end, her mom had a gigantic rummage sale at the farm and they'd been able to sell anything of value, including the items from her apartment. The rest was donated.

The bell above the door chimed and a group of four young men entered the store, laughing and joking with each other. The groom seemed reluctant but was trying to hide it. His smile seemed plastered on, his shoulders stiff, and though his friends all seemed to be enjoying the experience of finding their tuxedos, this poor young man didn't seem to be enjoying it at all. They pointed and touched a few of the tuxes, one of the guys pulled out a hideous tux decorated with cartoons all over it and between fits of laughter one of them said to the groom, "Let's surprise Amy with these on your wedding day."

The groom grinned but said nothing. Poor fella.

Which brought her thinking back to her own groom and where in the hell he was. Pulling her phone from her purse, she scrolled through her contacts and tapped Lincoln. Stepping from the tux store, she walked to her car as the ringing sounded in her ear. Three rings and a breathless Lincoln finally answered. "Hey Princess, what's up?"

"You sound out of breath, were you running?"

"No, I just apprehended a bounty, and he gave me a bit of a fight."

"Are you alright?"

He heaved out a loud breath, "Yeah." She heard him rustling a bit, then continue. "I'm just not as young as I used to be."

"That's true. You need to take care of yourself. Anyway, why are you apprehending a bounty when you're supposed to be getting fitted for a tux for the wedding."

"Uh." Silence. Even from the radio in his truck.

"Lincoln?"

"Ah, shit. I'm sorry Princess. I was on my way, honest. Then I saw Jeremy Piper, my bounty, leave the Copper Cup and I had to grab him. The scrawny shit took off running, and I had to catch him. I guess time got away from me."

Her nose wrinkled as she pursed her lips. Her mind raced to the young man in the tux shop now who didn't seem to want to get married at all and she wondered if Lincoln was subconsciously giving her clues.

"Lincoln, if you don't want to get married, we should talk about this."

"Where the hell did that come from? Please don't tell me you're getting all weird about the wedding. We've been under a lot of stress, but it'll get better. I just had an opportunity to bring in a couple thousand bucks and took it."

"I'm not weird, or getting weird. It just seemed as

though you'd forgotten that I was waiting here. And for that matter, Ford and Dodge aren't here either, so..."

"Shit." She heard more rustling, then his truck start up and the radio begin playing. The sound or noise of him placing his phone in the holder on the windshield and his Bluetooth taking over the call clicked in her ear. "Ford called and said he'd be a little late cause he's having a meeting with one of our Bond Agents who hasn't paid us. Dodge is coming in from out of town. He transferred a bounty to the Sheriff's Department for us."

"Okay. So, should I tell them inside that we need to reschedule?"

"No, I"m only about fifteen minutes away."

She glanced down at her shoes. Her sexy shoes. Her big purchase last month when she, Savannah and Megan went shopping for wedding accessories. She hadn't shown them to Lincoln; she wanted to surprise him with a nice dinner out tonight after getting his tuxedo fitted for the wedding. Since she'd been working for Big Three Bounty Hunting, she'd mostly worn jeans and t-shirts or pajama pants and t-shirts. She was always casual and missed dressing up now and then.

A truck came into the parking lot quickly and she chuckled when Dodge jumped out looking nervous. Almost like the groom inside.

"Okay. Dodge just pulled into the lot. I'll see you in a few minutes."

Tapping the end call icon, she tucked her phone inside her shoulder bag and turned to face Dodge. His shirt was ripped, he had a bruise on his jaw, his normally nonchalant expression was gone, and his brows were furrowed giving him a whole new appearance. The total look said "back off."

"What on earth happened to you?"

His head jerked back, then he looked down and tried in vain to straighten his shirt. When the ripped pocket on the front continued to droop, he shrugged and looked her in the eye. "Job hazard."

She inhaled a deep breath and mentally reminded herself this was her world now. Lincoln was always bruised, cut, or scraped; but he never complained. As a matter of fact, every time she asked him about the individual wounds on his body his smile would grow. And as he explained what happened, he grinned like a kid with a new toy. In the end, he always got his man and that made him happy.

She heard the bark of a dog and turned her head to see Abe's big head poking from the back window of Lincoln's truck as he pulled into the parking lot. She walked over and pet his beautiful head and earned a couple sloppy licks from him in return. They'd become best friends since she'd moved in with he and Lincoln.

Lincoln stepped from the truck, and her eyes quickly assessed his appearance. It was easy to stifle the sigh today because he didn't look much better than Dodge.

A smile grew on his face and the genuine love that showed in his eyes wiped away her doubt. "Good God Princess you look fantastic. To what do I owe the pleasure?"

He leaned down and wrapped his arms around her, pulling her tightly to him as he kissed her lips completely.

Her arms eagerly wrapped around his shoulders and she kissed him back. Normally, she'd wrap her legs around his waist, but she was wearing a pencil skirt and that didn't allow it. Plus, it was kind of slutty in public.

He gently set her on the ground then stood back, his brows raised.

"I wanted to take you out to dinner on a date after we were finished here. We haven't done that in a long time." She felt her hair to make sure it was still tucked neatly into her ponytail at the back of her head. "Actually, since we've been together, we've only been on one actual date."

His face relaxed as his eyes locked on hers. "Wow, you're right." He bent and scooped her into his arms, and began carrying her into the tux store. "Sexy shoes, Princess."

She giggled as she held her feet up to admire them herself.

"You can wear them tonight while I'm making love to you."

Dodge met them at the door and opened it for them. Lincoln whispered in her ear. "Only the shoes tonight. Nothing else."

30

CHANGE YOUR SHIRT

One date? What the hell was wrong with him? He should be treating her better than that. This woman deserved to be wined and dined. He smiled inwardly remembering that when he first met her, he thought she was used to Dom Perignon and caviar. She was a total surprise to him. Each night they sat out on the deck, drank a beer or a bourbon, and chatted about their day while watching Abe dive into the river and drag out sticks and debris. She laughed often, mothered him when he had a cut or a bruise, and fucked his brains out most nights.

But... "Princess, we can't go out to dinner tonight. Well, not just the two of us anyway. My sister Josie called and they're coming into town tonight."

"Josie, Seth and the kids?" She stiffened in his arms and he squeezed her closer.

"Just Josie and Seth. Both kids are still in college but will be here on Saturday for the wedding."

"Crap, the office is a mess at home and I didn't do the dishes before I came to town. She'll think I'm a terrible housekeeper. And since she decorated the place she'll have a bad image of me."

He kissed her temple, then gently set her down. He chuckled that she cared. "Honey, you haven't been to Josie's so you don't have a frame of reference, but a few things being out of place will not bother her. Not in the least. And they aren't staying with us anyway."

"What? Why are you making family stay in a hotel?"

"Because." His hands cupped her face and he stared deeply into the blue depths of her eyes. "Your family is staying at the hotel and so are mine. I don't want anyone staying with us. Not this time. Not when we're just settling ourselves. And certainly not on our wedding night."

Dodge stepped in next to Lincoln. "Pardon me for butting in on your little sweet talk session, but I need a shower and a nap. Can you show me what tux we're getting so I can get fitted and be on my way?"

Skye's brows rose and Lincoln grinned. She was about to dig into Dodge and he was going to enjoy it. "Do you have a romantic bone in your body? And why are you coming to get fitted for a tux when you need a shower? That's plain rude."

Yep, he knew it.

Dodge rubbed his bruised jaw and slowly answered her. "Darlin', I've already had a day from hell. My bounty, who was supposed to be easy, got in a few good punches before I tackled his ass and knocked him out. He ripped my favorite shirt which I put on for you. Then, the drive to the Sheriff's office over in South Pass was miserable due to road construction and a whiney bounty in the back fucking seat. Now my head is pounding and I want a shower, a beer, and a nap, probably in that order."

Skye slammed her hands on her hips and turned

slightly to face Lincoln. "You have to be more careful in apprehending your bounties. Both of you." She looked at him for good measure, and then turned back to Dodge. "I'll fix your shirt. You'll be able to have your beer and your nap after Ford gets here and you've been fitted."

The chime over the door sounded and a big brawny SEAL walked through it. Lincoln knew he was a SEAL instantly as his demeanor showed it. The way he walked with purpose and a no bullshit attitude. His high and tight haircut was a giveaway. But not to be too cocky, he wore a t-shirt that said Navy. No way he was a seaman.

He walked into the store and bold as can be said, "Hey there beautiful, care to help me learn how to dress?"

Skye spun around and in a flash she was across the store and flying into his big beefy arms. To say Lincoln's stomach knotted up was an understatement. The SEAL's arms wrapped around her, and Lincoln could see from his vantage point just how slender Skye was. Maybe he should fatten her up a bit so other brawny men didn't take so kindly to her.

Now here he stood watching his future wife hug another man, one he was admittedly jealous of, and he didn't know what to do. He glanced at Dodge who stood watching the whole thing with disbelief on his face. And if his balled fists were an indication, he was about ready to get his clock kicked. Again.

The SEAL set his Princess down and when she turned and looked at him, the happiness on her face was like a punch to the gut. Until she said, "Linc, honey, this is my brother, Logan."

Shit, he should have put that together in two seconds. Idiot. He shook his head quickly to clear his thoughts as he walked forward to shake his future brother-in-law's hand.

Logan chuckled and Lincoln realized he probably looked like he wanted to brawl while Skye was hugging him. Shaking hands, they both offered a firm grip, the way men size each other up when meeting. It must be some stupid ancient ritual from back in the day trying to show who's stronger or in charge. Lincoln shook his head again and was thrilled to see up close he was actually an inch taller than Logan. Winner.

"Nice to meet you, Logan. We weren't expecting you today, but I'm glad you're able to make it."

"I wouldn't miss Skye getting married for the world. That tool she was married to before treated her like shit, so I came before the wedding to make sure you weren't going to do the same thing. Gotta take care of my baby sister."

"Logan!" Skye scolded.

Lincoln chuckled as he pulled her close. "Don't scold Princess. It's what any good man should do."

He looked back at Dodge. "Dodge, come and meet Logan."

The two shook hands and he watched Skye's face, which now took on a happy glow and it made his heart swell a bit.

The door chimed again and Ford entered, looking a bit irritated but nonetheless he was here. Making a quick introduction to Logan, he then turned to Skye. "We're all here so let's get our tuxes fitted and ordered so Dodge can nap."

She giggled, took his hand, and walked them to the far wall where the tuxes were lined up in various styles and colors. She pointed out a couple she liked and honestly, he'd wear anything she asked him to wear to get married. Except the ascot, he wasn't an ascot man. Nope.

The selection was made and Dodge and Ford left. "So Logan, my sister Josie and her husband Seth will be landing at the airport in about a half hour. They're staying at the Mountain House Inn, where the wedding reception is, would you like to go and have a drink there in the bar while we wait for them?"

"That sounds great."

Skye asked, "Logan, how did you know where we'd be?"

"Mom." He chuckled. "I called her when I got off the plane to get their new address and she told me you were getting tuxes today and I could save you a second trip to the tux store if I came here first.

Skye laughing was a magnificent sound. Her face was radiant, her eyes were bright and her smile, well there was nothing better than that. "That's mom for you. Okay, let's make our way to the hotel."

Lincoln kissed her at the driver's door of her car. "I'll be there soon, but I'm going to take Abe home first Princess and that will give you a little time with Logan. I'll be there in about twenty minutes."

"Okay, but no more bounties today. And maybe you can change your shirt. Pretty please." She kissed his lips and he decided changing his shirt wasn't that big of a deal, so he'd do it. He was in deep.

31

WHAT HAVE YOU PLANNED?

"When's Savannah arriving?"

Savannah lived in Minneapolis where she was climbing the corporate ladder. Skye used to think that's what she wanted too, but when she and Lincoln met, she realized she had been looking for the wrong kind of life with the wrong kind of man.

"She'll be here tomorrow evening. You know Savannah, she wants to take the least amount of time off of work that she can." They both laughed.

Logan leaned forward, "I think I'm getting out, Skye. This contract is up in three months and I'm giving it some serious thought."

"Wow, Logan, I love the idea of you being able to come home more often, or possibly live here, but I thought you loved being a SEAL."

"I do, sis. It's just after all the shit went down with you and mom and dad, I can't help feeling as if I should have been here. You were working your fingers to the bone taking care of them and the farm and it almost got you killed. Dad's accident left him forever physically changed and I wasn't here to help with any of it. There comes a time when a man has to grow the fuck up and do what's right, not what he wants."

"Oh, honey, life is long and if you're doing something you don't want to do, it's not a good life. Plus you're helping to keep us all safe by doing what you do."

He took a drink from his beer glass and sat back. "I know. And for a long time I did what I wanted and needed to do. But, it's a hard life, Skye. And, I think at 46 years old, I'm finally ready to do something else."

"Like what?"

"I don't know. Maybe I'll talk Lincoln into letting me be a bounty hunter or something."

She giggled. "No doubt you'd be good at it and they have so much work. But, you need to think long and hard about that. Both Lincoln and Dodge have bruised jaws today due to bounties they were rounding up. It's not always easy."

"Sweetheart, I didn't say I was looking for something easy."

Her chair tilted back and she squealed. Lincoln bent over her and kissed her lips. Righted her chair then addressed Logan. "What are you drinking Logan, I'll get another."

"Take a seat, Lincoln and watch this." Logan's grin was huge as he winked at her.

"Oh, God, he's so impressed with himself." She whispered to Lincoln.

Logan raised his hand and a dark-haired waitress, the same one who first served them and simpered profusely over Logan, practically ran to their table. Logan smiled his best smile and winked at her. "We'll have another round here. Linc, what'll you have?"

She watched Lincoln try not to smile, but the truth of the matter was, this probably happened to him all the time too. "I'll have the same thing Logan's drinking."

"Coming right up. Anything else I can get you?" That question was aimed directly at Logan. Subtle.

"Not right now darlin', but possibly later."

She almost squealed before turning and using an exaggerated sway, sauntered away. Good God.

"I love Lynyrd Station." Logan said.

Lincoln chuckled and shook his head.

"Josie just called and they're on their way here. Where would you like to eat?" He lay his hand over hers on the table and she wanted to melt at the look in his eyes.

"I'm in the mood for meat." Her cheeks instantly brightened as his brows rose into the lock of dark hair that fell onto his forehead, and the double entendre flowed over her. "I meant steak, a big thick juicy steak."

Lincoln winked at her and luckily she was saved from further embarrassment as a tall, slender female version of Lincoln called out from the doorway as she hustled toward them.

"Linc!"

She was breathtaking. Her long dark hair hung in curls over one shoulder and already from this distance Skye could see she had eyes the same or similar to Lincoln's smokey gray. Her husband was broad shouldered and close in height to his wife, but he also commanded attention and the two of them together - wow was the only word that came to mind.

She swallowed to moisten her throat which had grown dry and subconsciously wiped her palms on her thighs.

Lincoln walked around the table to greet his sister and he did so enthusiastically. Lifting her off the ground and hugging her close, the smile on his gorgeous face was sigh worthy. Of course it always was. Lincoln's brother-in-law, Seth, stepped around the hugging siblings and headed her way. His smile was wide in his handsome face. He stretched his hand out to shake hers and the instant their hands connected, his free hand clasped over hers.

"It's a pleasure to meet you Skye; Lincoln has told us so much about you."

It was impossible not to like him, and her smile felt genuine, not stiff as she worried it would be when she responded. "It's a pleasure to meet you too. And Lincoln's been very busy filling everyone in on everyone else."

He chuckled and stepped back as Josie came to stand in front of her, grabbed both of her shoulders in her hands and stared at her. "You are as gorgeous as Linc said you were and your pictures don't do you justice. I understand why he calls you Princess. You're a real life Cinderella."

She then pulled Skye to her in a bear hug that felt genuine and loving. When Josie pulled back, her eyes floated to Logan. "Well now, who do we have here?"

Skye giggled, "This is my brother Logan."

They shook hands and immediately additional chairs were added to the table for the group to sit.

Josie chimed right in, "I need to know everything about the wedding. What's gone on with the planning, where is it to be held, how many people, everything."

Skye's head spun as the indomitable Josie seemed to take charge. "Well, um, I'm afraid..."

Josie continued, "Oh, sorry to interrupt but I must say, I'm very sorry I haven't been more involved with the planning. That hotel job I had took up every spare moment, but it turned out fantastic."

Lincoln saved Skye from having to apologize for the simple planning they'd done. "Josie, calm down. We aren't having a huge, elaborate wedding. I've told you that." He looked at Skye and took her hand which settled her nerves. "Skye and I have been through so much in the past few months and so have her parents. Together we decided to keep things simple and low-key."

"There's nothing wrong with simple and low-key Linc and I don't care at all about that. I'm just excited for you and Skye, and I want to know what you've planned."

32

WE ALL PROMISED

Lincoln woke and brushed the sleep from his eyes with his fingers. The last two days were a blur. Josie, as much as he loved her, was a force for certain. She kept them hopping every day keeping things on track. When he'd kissed Skye goodbye last night, something he didn't want to do, but Josie insisted was for good luck, she looked exhausted. The only thing that helped him get to sleep was Ford's best bourbon and finally having some quiet time.

So, here he lay, alone in bed at Ford and Megan's and all he wanted to do was run down the mountain and kiss his future bride before the ceremony. He guessed she was feeling very much the same, but leaving her at their house last night, with her sister who finally arrived five minutes before the rehearsal, made him feel a bit better. They had catching up to do. Today, though, Savannah was moving to the Inn where the rest of both of their families were staying and tonight, he'd be in bed with his beautiful, perfect wife. Just a few more hours.

Abe stretched then came to the side of the bed and

rested his chin on the mattress, looking for a little affection. Lincoln patted the bed and Abe eagerly jumped up
and licked his face, his wicked tail slapping the bed in his
excitement.

"She'll be ours in a little while, Abe."

Abe's tail rapidly wagged and he earned a few more
licks on the cheek.

Patting his head once more, he kissed his pup's head
and rolled away. A quick glance at his phone told him it
was still early about six a.m. Early but he knew Ford was
probably already up.

Rubbing his hands down his face to wake-up, he
reached for his pajama pants laying at the end of the bed
and slipped his feet into them one at a time. Standing and
pulling them up, he then snagged his t-shirt from the bed
and picked up his phone as he headed to the door.

Quiet as a mouse he ascended the steps one at a time
so he didn't wake Shelby, Abe at his side. At the top of the
stairs he could see across the living room to Ford staring at
his computer, the steam from his coffee still billowing
from his black cup. Ford's brows were furrowed, his jaw
tight.

He walked to the front door and let Abe out to do his
business. Deciding to get his own coffee before speaking,
he walked to the kitchen counter and grinned when he
saw that Ford had already set out a cup for him. Pouring
his coffee and adding cream, he picked up his cup and
walked to the living area, which conveniently was next to
Ford's desk. The open concept of this house meant you
could stand in the kitchen and still be in the living room
and Ford's office. Just the opposite of his home but it
worked. Up here, the views were breathtaking and able to
be seen from every room.

Sitting on the sofa sipping his hot brew he swallowed then decided to interrupt his friend's reading.

"Looks like bad news."

"Yes and no. Just got some intelligence that says Mangus is still trafficking art and jewels. That could mean guns, too, since he used the art and jewels as cover for the guns in the past, though that was Victor's game. But Mangus has a love of jewels and art and it seems even the recent heat and closing of Limitless here in Lynyrd Station hasn't slowed him down. And he's still doing it from Lynyrd Station."

"He's one stupid fucker. With the feds crawling all over Lynyrd Station he either hasn't had time to move operations. Doesn't have any other place to move them since the feds are now crawling all over the California operations. Or he enjoys the game."

Ford finally looked over at him. "I think it's a combination of all three of those things. This intelligence from Lynyrd Station PD says a shipment came in at three this morning via a white van from the south. Once it entered the general vicinity, their intelligence lost it."

Lincoln took a deep breath and let it out slowly. "So recent activity means there will probably be a shipment out later today if he follows Victor's former pattern."

"Right."

Both men sat still pondering what this meant. Normally they'd spring into action, hunker down where their reports said the last sighting was, and where they had some information where the Santarino operations were hiding. But, their hands were tied. He was getting married in six hours. And, he promised Skye he wouldn't come to the church covered in new bruises and cuts.

"Linc, Dodge and I can run down and see what we can

find out. We'll be back in time to shower and change for the wedding. You can stay here, relax, and practice your vows; you don't want to fuck up."

"That's such bullshit. I'm not going to sit here like a pampered dog while you and Dodge are out there following that bastard. I can go too. The three of us can cover more ground and still be back in time to shower and get to the church."

"Linc, you can't be late or scuffed up. We all heard you promise Skye last night and we all promised your wedding pictures wouldn't be full of men who looked like they'd been brawling."

"If it's just recon, we won't be bruised up." Abe came to the patio doors just behind Ford's desk and his friend jumped up to let him in.

"I'd like to see what we can find. There's some money in it for us and since we haven't been paid for the last three bounties we've picked up from Santana Jones, I'd like to make some cash we can count on."

"I thought you went and talked with Jones about not paying us." Lincoln finished his coffee and set his cup on the coffee table before him.

"I did and he told me he'd have the money to me yesterday, but of course he didn't show up." Ford finished his coffee then sat back in his chair.

"Okay, give Dodge a call and I'll run down and get dressed. The sooner we head out the sooner we'll be back."

He hustled down stairs and as excited as he was to marry Skye, he was eager to finish this mission to ensure they all got paid, now that the feds and Lynyrd Station PD authorized Big Three to continue to help them ascertain how this operation was continuing to operate. He planned on taking Skye to Hawaii after they finished with Santarino and while they had a healthy bank account. It rankled to think they'd been working for free.

Quickly pulling on the jeans and t-shirt he wore over here last night, he slipped his feet into his tennis shoes as Abe began excitedly pacing. As he bent to tie his shoes his phone sounded the text alert. Pulling it off the night stand he read, "*I love you and I can't wait to be Mrs. Lincoln Winter.*"

He swallowed the guilt clawing its way up his throat. It would be alright; it was just recon. He quickly texted a reply. "*I love you too and can't wait to call you my wife.*"

He couldn't stop the grin on his face as he thought about life with Skye. She was simply everything he'd ever dreamed his wife would be but didn't think that person was alive. Life was funny about dropping people in your lap when you least expected it.

Leaving the bedroom, he glanced quickly at his tuxedo hanging in front of the closet. He'd be back in time and without bruises as he promised. He had to.

33

LINCOLN ENTERTAINS ME

Skye soaked in the tub for twenty minutes. The water was still warm, thanks to Lincoln's fore-thought in adding a heated soaking tub. But she just couldn't relax, today was her wedding day. She read the text from Lincoln again and smiled. Life was good.

She'd hated being in their bed alone last night. Her time with Savannah was so infrequent that she was thrilled to have it, but she wanted Lincoln there with her. Typical new bride.

Wrapping herself in the big, pink fluffy robe Lincoln bought her when he'd laid eyes on her old ratty robe, she inhaled and closed her eyes. She could smell his after shave on it. He loved hugging her when she wore this robe. Then he loved taking it off of her. Her nipples pebbled at the thought. Had it only been one night?

Leaving the bathroom, she heard her email chime as she passed the office. Looking for something to take her mind off of how many hours before she was Mrs. Winter, she stepped into the office and sat at her desk. Lifting the lid on her laptop, she opened her email program and saw there were several emails from Jared Timm. She clicked the first one open, which was from three o'clock this morning.

From: Jared Timm

Date: June 23, 2018 - 03:36 a.m.

To: Lincoln Winter; Ford Montgomery; Dodge Sager

Cc: Skye Sommers

Santarino sighting driving up Ryker Mountain. Driving a black Ford F-150, about 9 years old or so. He seemed to disappear into the mountain. I'm still watching the area.

I've copied Skye on this email so she has my latest invoice - attached.

Jared

She looked at the time again and unease clawed at her stomach. Knowing the Big Three like she did, this was dangling bait and they wouldn't be able to resist. Deciding to get a cup of coffee and not dwell on this too much, she closed the lid on her laptop and walked down the hall to the kitchen. The house was quiet at just after 6:00 a.m. Normally Lincoln would already be up and her coffee would be sitting on the night stand when she woke. Abe would be bounding around eager to go to work. There was activity. Today, the quiet made her stomach twist.

Savannah was still sleeping, so she pulled her phone from the pocket of her robe and tapped the icon for her mom. She was surely awake by now.

"Hi honey, what are you doing up so early?"

She smiled as her mother's chipper demeanor seeped into her dark thoughts. "I couldn't sleep. I've already soaked in the tub and checked my email."

"Is Savannah still sleeping?"

"Yeah. We stayed awake until midnight catching up.

I've missed her."

"Me too, sweetheart. Tonight it's my turn to stay up late with her after we leave the reception."

"I'm glad you'll have that time before she goes back on Monday."

She could hear her mother cluck her tongue like she did when one of her children needed her. "So what's wrong, baby?"

Oh, stupid tears raced to her eyes hearing her mom's concern. She'd put them through far too much in recent months. But, she needed to talk to someone. "I saw an email alerting Lincoln and the guys to a sighting of a Santarino shipment. I'm afraid they won't be able to resist and will take off on a mission this morning and miss our wedding."

Her mother chuckled. "Skye, that man loves you so much. He promised you that he wouldn't get married with bruises." She could hear her mom sip from her coffee cup and it was comforting, the familiar sounds of home. "Besides, what if he did come to the wedding with a bruise or a cut? Would you call it off?"

"No, of course not."

"Would it make you love him less?"

"No, mom, no."

"So, he's a man who wants to keep the woman he loves safe. Mangus Santarino and those minions who work for him are a danger to you since Victor's death. At least that's what Lincoln thinks. If he takes an opportunity to try and protect you, I think that's about the sweetest wedding gift a woman could ever receive. How about you?"

She watched the water of the river flow by the house out the kitchen windows, the tears in her eyes blurring the beauty of the gorgeous spring day. Her wedding day.

"When you put it like that, I'd say it's the best wedding gift ever."

Her mom giggled and then sighed. Silly woman. "I'm pretty lucky aren't I, mom?"

"Oh sweetheart, you are the luckiest woman alive."

Savannah shuffled into the kitchen, her short blonde hair standing up at funny angles, her eyes still puffy from sleep, and a frown on her face. She never was a happy person in the morning.

"I've got to go mom, the morning monster just walked into the kitchen and I better fill her with coffee before she tears my head off."

Her mom laughed and Savannah gave her the finger. "No fighting girls, see you in a couple of hours."

"Bye mom."

Laying her phone on the counter she turned and pulled a coffee cup from the cupboard above the coffee pot. Savannah shuffled to the table and plopped down into a chair with about as much grace as a cow.

Setting her coffee in front of her, Skye sat next to her sister and watched the river flow by. They sat in silence for a few moments before Savannah finally broke the silence. "You have a great place here, sis."

"Yeah."

More silence as Savannah drained her cup, got another, refilled her cup then sat again. Sipping loudly, she finally smiled. "I don't know how you can stand living out here in the boonies with no movie shows for miles, no five star restaurants, and no venues for theater productions. Boring."

Ah, that's when she looked at her sister and sighed. "Lincoln entertains me in ways that would curl your toes and that's more than enough for me."

34

THE PAIN WOULD BEGIN KICKING
HIS ASS

Lincoln found himself crouching behind a large mass of shrubbery on the side of Ryker Mountain. His knees hurt from being frozen in the same position for what felt like hours. His headset chirped and Ford called out. "No sighting here and it's been two hours. I think we call it and wait until we have a timeline from Jared as to Columbus' comings and goings."

Columbus, the code name they used for Santarino. Still made him chuckle every time.

He responded, "I'm good with that. I've got a wedding to get ready for."

Dodge called out, "Roger that, I'm ready. My ass is sore, my knees are aching, and my shoulders are screaming out for blood."

Lincoln shook his head and chuckled as he began following his trail down the side of the mountain. The rocky terrain made it easy to climb undetected by a trail, but it was difficult navigating the rocks and slippery moss that covered some of the stones.

A sharp pain laced through his left shoulder and his

footing slipped. He found himself falling forward and was only able to twist his body enough to make sure he didn't land on his face on the rocks, but his back took the brunt of his fall and the wind sailed from his lungs.

His vision was hazy and dark and he consciously had to will himself to not panic as he struggled to breathe. Hearing footsteps come toward him, he tried once again to catch a breath and was able to finally take in air. Blinking rapidly to clear his vision, he looked up to see one of Santarino's men making his way down the mountain to where he lay now. The club he carried in his hand must have been what Lincoln had been hit with. Thank God for adrenaline because his was kicking in right now in spades.

He sat up, not without groaning, hit the button on his ear piece. "I need help here, I'm under attack. One that I can see."

He rolled to the side, grabbed a large rock for leverage, and managed to hoist himself up. He wheezed as his lungs completely refilled with air and pain shot through his shoulder. He watched his attacker come closer and he wasn't sure if he should stay and fight or try to make his way down the mountain. He reached behind him to grab his gun from his inside holster, only to realize it was gone. Fighting the urge to look around so his new companion didn't realize he wasn't armed, he decided to look him in the eye and keep himself behind the rock until Dodge or Ford could get here.

Dodge came from the left of his assailant and almost at the same level on the mountain. The distraction was enough for his new enemy to turn his head. Lincoln took that moment to look around at where he landed. His gun lay nestled between the rocks which meant he'd have to bend over to retrieve it. The thought almost made him cringe. He'd been injured worse before.

Within a minute, the glint of the sun on metal caught his eye and he saw his foe pull a gun from his waistband and point it at Dodge. Dodge grabbed for his own gun, but without thought Lincoln reached down, grabbed his from its resting place, aimed, and shot his enemy. He got him in the thigh, and the man dropped like a rock which allowed Dodge to jump on him and take his gun away. While their injured attacker howled and then began a stream of curse words in Italian, Ford arrived lower on the mountain. He stared up at them, saw they were both okay, and let out a breath. Pulling his phone from his back pocket, he tapped his phone a couple of times then put it to his ear.

"Rory, I need an ambulance and assistance on the North side of Ryker Mountain. One man down, shot in the thigh." Pulling his phone from his ear he looked up at both of them.

Lincoln nodded, then began his descent down the rest of the mountain side. Without another word Ford continued on his call, "Another ambulance for one of mine."

Ford pocketed his phone and watched as Lincoln made his way slowly, carefully selecting where to place his feet. The sharp pain in his shoulder and back with every movement made him long for pain killers and booze.

"Is Skye going to ream my ass out for not keeping you at home this morning? You look like shit."

"To be honest, I'm beginning to feel like shit. Bastard hit me with a club in the shoulder and I fell landing on my back. But, if you can tape and drug me up, she won't need to know until later."

Dodge caught up to him and chuckled, "I doubt she'll miss how your moving, Linc. Prepare to get your ass reamed." He scoffed then finished with, "Women."

Dodge stepped just in front of him then stopped and patted his own shoulder. "Hang on to me and I'll get you down from this rocky piece of shit."

He would have told him to go to hell, but he felt like he was already in it. The pain shooting through his back with every breath just about blacked him out. Likely he had a broken rib or two. Figures. He was going to be in big trouble for certain. The only thing Skye asked of him was not to come to the wedding all beat up. And he'd promised her. Promised. What was he if he couldn't even keep a fucking promise?

Embracing the pain because honestly at this point he felt he deserved it, he held on to Dodge's shoulder and allowed his friend to guide him along. Probably never hear the end of this either.

Once they reached bottom, they could hear the sirens as they grew closer. And right now, the thought of laying down in an ambulance and taking a bit of a nap sounded pretty fucking appealing. He snaked his phone from his front pocket and glanced at the time. Almost ten o'clock. He had an hour before he had to be at the church to get ready and have pictures taken. He needed a shower, drugs, and to be taped up. In that order.

The first car that reached them was Rory's followed closely by two ambulances, and Lincoln nearly cried at the sight. Relief was almost here. As his adrenaline left his body, the pain increased and one misstep sent pain slicing through his back. His shoulder throbbed and, he had to admit, he was beginning to feel queasy. Last thing he wanted was to throw up.

The EMTs ran to him while his friends pointed out the injured man up on the side of the mountain to Rory and his team.

"Sir, tell me where you're injured."

He tried taking a deep breath which was a huge mistake. The white hot pain shot through him and his head swam. Softly he whispered, "Lower back, I think a rib and my left shoulder. I was hit with a club or something."

The EMTs slowly removed his shirt and began their inspection of his injuries. "I can give you something for pain, but it's temporary."

"Temporary works."

One EMT jumped into the back of the ambulance and prepared something for him which he hoped worked fast.

"I'm getting married in two hours, so you need to work fast here."

"I'm not sure that's advisable..."

"Advisable or not, it's going to happen. So, we need to move."

Ford stepped up to them at that moment his dark brooding eyes taking in everything. "I can call Skye, Linc and tell her what happened."

"No." It was hard getting the word from his mouth. He felt a pinch, then a tingle, and soon he felt. Nothing. Nice.

"I need a shower, so whatever you wrap me up in needs to come off and then get re-wrapped."

"But sir..."

Dodge chuckled, "Don't bother folks. He's got himself a hot little wife-to-be and he doesn't want to disappoint her. Even though she'd understand." Lincoln felt a bit guilty at the admonition in his friend's eyes; but he just couldn't let Skye down and all of their guests. It was too much.

Ford stepped forward and helped him out. "My wife's a nurse and she can help to re-bandage him after his shower. So if you can get him fixed up enough to get him home, we'll figure it out from there."

Ford ruffled his hair like he was a little boy, and he had to admit he didn't even mind it. Now he just had to get ready to get to church and get through the ceremony before the pain began kicking his ass again.

35

YOU'RE LINCOLN'S PRINCESS

Skye carried her wedding dress, all neatly tucked into the white garment bag, into the back of the church. Savannah, Josie, and Megan were behind her chatting away about what she didn't know. Her stomach was in knots and her throat was dry, hopefully she wasn't getting sick.

Her mom walked ahead of her, carrying her own dress and a large bag slung over her shoulder, with Lincoln's mom, who had arrived late last night due to cancelled flights and airport screwups. Luckily, she was the kind of person to blow it off and not let it ruin her weekend. She smiled as she watched the two moms chat on about their children as children and compare notes as to how soon they hoped for grandchildren and long visits. They weren't even married and, in the very church where the ceremony was to happen, these two were already talking about grandchildren. Both women were already grandmothers, but it was natural to always want more. Or so her mom had told her often.

Reaching the room at the far end of the hallway, her mom opened the door, and held it for all the girls to enter.

The florescent lights flickered on, and the room felt a bit cool right now, but she'd probably be sweating from nerves soon. She'd prided herself just this week, and again this morning, on her composure and how everything had just pulled together nicely without any drama. It must be meant to be.

Hanging her dress on the back of a closet door, she unzipped the bag and fluffed her dress up to keep it from wrinkling. The large bag her mom had slung over her shoulder was deposited on a table; and to her disbelief, her mom pulled out an iron, a spray bottle, a box of bobby pins, combs and brushes, makeup mirrors, and her makeup.

"Mom, good gravy, did you pack the whole house?"

Melissa clucked her tongue, "We need to be prepared sweetheart."

Her bridesmaids did the same with the bags they carried; and she looked over the plethora of makeup, hair spray, makeup brushes, and so much more. "This place could rival the makeup counter at Nieman Marcus." She mused.

Josie, ever the organizer, started with instructions. "Skye, the photographer will be here in twenty minutes to begin taking pictures of us getting ready. So, how dressed do you want to be when he gets here?"

"Ah..." Her mind went blank. How dressed? "Dressed, I guess."

"Okay, then let's get you in your dress." Josie walked to the gorgeous white dress hanging just behind her and began looking it over. "Melissa, there are a couple of wrinkles in the back here, do you think you can press them out?"

"Oh, of course."

Skye looked at the spot where Josie pointed and didn't see a wrinkle. Looking into her future sister-in-law's eyes her brows furrowed. Josie winked then whispered, "We have to keep the moms busy or they'll fuss. This will give them something to focus on so we can all get ready without their nerves taking over and making all of us nervous."

Skye smiled and whispered back, "You're brilliant."

"I've dealt with hundreds of people when designing their homes. I've learned if I give them something to do, I get my own work done without answering a thousand questions."

Taking Skye's arm, she gently pulled her to the table piled high with makeup. "Put your makeup on, Princess, my brother is waiting to make you his wife."

"Is this your ploy to keep me busy so I don't let my nerves get the better of me."

"Yes."

She promptly trotted out the door but returned within a couple of minutes with a white box from the florist in town. Setting the box at the end of the table she looked at Megan and Savannah. "Ladies, can you help me sort these flowers so we know which ones go upstairs to the men and which stay down here? There should be labels on them with names."

Without question the two women began marveling at the flowers and doing as they were told. Josie was positively brilliant with this. Everyone was busy, happily chatting, and enjoying the day. She'd have to remember this for future use.

A knock at the door had Josie hustling across the floor. "Hi."

"I need to speak with Megan please."

It was Ford. Skye stood to lock eyes with Ford only to see him quickly look away from her. Alarm bells rang in her head. "Ford?"

"Ah, I just need to see Megan for a minute, Skye. It's about Shelby."

Megan stepped out into the hall with her husband. Within a minute she poked her head in the room and said, "I'll be right back, I have to ahh ...attend to something. For Shelby. I'll be back."

She quickly closed the door and Skye swallowed the lump in her throat. Something was wrong. She looked to her mom and found her mom looking at her, her lips sucked between her teeth. "Don't get yourself riled up, sweetheart, you have no idea it's anything other than what Megan said."

Josie came to her side, "My brother loves you. There's nothing going on. Finish your makeup please."

She stared into her future sister-in-law's eyes, so similar to Lincoln's and her stomach twisted again. "Something's wrong."

"You don't know that. For all we know, Shelby had an epic diaper accident and the babysitter doesn't know what to do."

"The babysitter is Ford's sister who has children of her own and knows what to do."

Josie sat in the chair next to her while pulling her down into her own, took one of Skye's hands into hers, and looked deep into her eyes. "It's fine. Please don't worry and get yourself ready before the photographer gets here.

If you want me to, I'll call Lincoln and make sure he's alright."

All she could do was nod. Swallowing the giant lump in her throat, she watched as Josie pulled her phone from her back pocket, tapped a couple of times, scrolled, and tapped again before putting the phone to her ear. "Linc, I'm just calling to make sure everything is alright. Skye's worried because Ford came down to get Megan."

Josie listened but her eyes never left the table in front of her and that also worried Skye. She should just go upstairs and make sure he's alright herself. Ever since she'd read Jared Timm's email, she'd had this sick feeling in the pit of her stomach. She'd tamped it down most of the morning, but now it was growing and she was losing control of it.

"Okay. Great, I'll see you in about forty-five minutes."

She ended the call and tucked her phone into her pocket. "He's fine, they're upstairs getting ready right now. The photographer just left and is on his way down here. Do you want to slip into your dress before he gets here?"

Nodding, she glanced in the mirror once more, her makeup was close to being finished. She just wanted to brush her teeth first, then put her lipstick on, but that could wait.

Standing, she walked across the room to where her mom and future mom were fussing over her dress and gabbing about what their grandchildren would look like. Shaking her head, she asked, "Is it ready for me to put on?"

"Yes, dear." Her mom stood straight and played with the lace brocade on the dress. "Okay, get your jeans and shirt off."

Lincoln's mom, Betty, began unpinning her slip from the hanger as Skye slipped out of her clothing. She'd donned her strapless bra and pretty lacy panties this morning and now she was a bit embarrassed for their mothers to see her undergarments. To her surprise Betty kept her back turned and busied herself while her mother fussed with straightening her dress out to be stepped into. Betty quickly handed her the half-slip, then made herself busy with the hanger and bag. Skye stepped into her slip which made her feel a little less exposed.

Her mom held her dress open for her to step into and Betty offered her a hand as she put first one foot then the other inside her dress. Each mom took a side gently pulling it up, helping her slip her arms into the little lace cap sleeves, then zipping up the back. Turning she looked into the full-length mirror and her eyes welled with tears. She'd loved this dress when she first found it and looking at it now, well she loved it even more. The narrow lace cap sleeves slipped sexily off her shoulders. The sweetheart bodice showed only a hint of cleavage, but a hint was much sexier than a lot. The white-lace adorned dress was fitted from the top to her thighs where it lightly flared out; patches of lace decorated the tulle here and there and trimmed the entire hem and train. She felt like the princess Lincoln thought she was.

She'd opted for a flat veil to lay on her hair and no jewelry because she wanted the focus to be on her dress. The smile that appeared on its own told her she'd chosen well.

"Oh, honey. You're simply beautiful." Her mom whispered as tears filled her eyes. Savannah came to stand on her other side. She was struck with the memory that they hadn't had a picture of only the three of them since her first wedding and that had been a rushed, hurried affair. This felt calm, serene, and simply perfect.

"We need this picture." She whispered it as she took in the way the three of them looked standing together. Her long blonde hair fell in waves around her shoulders while her sister's slightly darker blonde hair was spiked out in a frisky do that she wore so very well. Their mother was a couple of inches shorter than she and Savannah; her short neat graying hair fit her petite face just perfectly. And though they all looked a bit different, they were so similar it was striking.

Josie broke into her musings. "Good, let's start with that."

She waved to the door and the photographer entered the room stopping to set numerous camera bags on one of the tables and moved to stand before them. He reached out and shook their hands. "Tom Chatten, nice to meet you."

Josie took the reins once again; Skye realized what Lincoln had meant when he said she'd take charge, but Skye was so happy to allow it. "Let's start with pictures of the bride with her mom and her sister. Then I'd like my mom and I with Skye. Then the bridesmaids, then all of us together. Then I'll go upstairs and we can get a couple of pictures of me pinning Lincoln's boutonnière on. Then we can get these two married."

Tom grinned and began snapping photos asking them to change position here and there. Megan rushed in while they were snapping photos with Josie, Betty and Skye. She looked flustered and avoided eye contact which further set Skye's nerves on edge.

Megan grabbed her dress off the rail it was hanging on and ducked out to the bathroom in the hallway. Absently biting her lip, Tom interrupted Skye, "Can't have the bride looking pensive, Skye."

She smiled but it didn't reach her eyes. She absently thought of two things. She hoped Lincoln was alright and she'd probably look at these pictures and see the worry on her face, but that couldn't be helped.

Megan rushed back in and Tom kept them busy snapping pictures. Then Betty approached her with a beautifully wrapped package and told her, "This is from Josie and I as our gift to you, Skye."

Her fingers shook as she tried to untie the gorgeous light pink bow while the girls all laughed. Pulling the top off the silver wrapped box with tiny pink and deep gray hearts on it, the sparkle that peeked through the light pink tissue paper made her suck in her breath. Gently pulling the tissue paper back, she revealed a beautiful crown of crystals.

"You're Lincoln's princess, so we thought you should wear a crown." Betty said.

36

HE'D BE GETTING AN ASS CHEWING

Josie pinned his boutonnière onto his lapel as he kept his breathing shallow. "I'd kill you myself if I didn't think Skye deserved the honor. What the hell were you thinking, Linc?"

"I thought it was just recon...."

"No, you don't get to do that. You made a promise to Skye. Much like the one you're about to make before our families. How can she believe you when you say you'll love, honor and obey?"

He closed his eyes and willed his heartbeat to slow as the guilt once again washed over him. Luckily Dodge stepped in to help him. "Josie, quit busting his balls. We thought we'd just go and do a little recon work. It would pass the morning and we'd have a little work to show for it. And, please remember, Linc wants the Santarino clan out of Lynyrd Station sooner rather than later. We all do. So, we'd hoped we'd be one step closer. We never dreamed we'd be ambushed."

Lincoln locked eyes with Dodge and watched his friend grin. He was enjoying his ass chewing far too much.

Josie stood back, hands on her hips, and scowled at him. He braced himself for more ranting. To his surprise she said, "How badly hurt are you?"

"Two broken ribs and a badly bruised shoulder. I'll be fine. I've been worse."

"Not on your wedding night you haven't. Good luck consummating your marriage tonight, big guy." She stepped back, grabbed the empty boutonniere box, and headed to the door. "Big dumbass," she muttered on her way out.

He looked at his friends and his future brother-in-law and whispered, "That wasn't too bad."

Logan laughed, "You haven't had to deal with Skye or Mom yet, so don't go getting all cocky yet."

The pastor entered the room, "We're about to start the ceremony. Are you ready, Lincoln?"

"Yes." He slowly inhaled to fill his lungs as much as he could and let it out. He nodded to his groomsmen, and then followed pastor out of the room behind the pulpit. He took his place at the end of the aisle. His guys extra space followed him out, but then walked down the aisle so each could escort a bridesmaid to the altar.

If he could change the events of the morning, he would do it in a heartbeat. Not because of how he felt now, but because of the one person who meant the world to him that he didn't want to disappoint. Skye. Sadly, he was about to disappoint her, it killed him a little imagining the look on her face when she realized he'd broken his promise to her. Josie was right, he was a big dumbass.

The music volume increased and the doors at the back of the church opened. Megan and Ford began their descent down the aisle, and he assumed they were thinking of their own wedding not so long ago. He ventured a glance into the congregation and his brother, Aaron, winked at him. His niece, Jessica, all grown up and pretty, sat with her father, the look on her face part happy and part holding back tears. The last time they were in church together was when Aaron's wife and Jessica's mother was laid to rest after a car accident.

Glancing across the church Skye's brother Devin, his wife, and their children sat neatly dressed with smiles on their faces. She had a great family. Melissa waved to him, the smile on her face as bright as the sun. Then he glanced over at his mom and dad earning smiles and a wink from his dad.

Ford kissed Megan at the end of the aisle and came to stand next to him fist bumping him as he passed.

Josie began walking down the aisle with Dodge next. The agreement Lincoln and Skye came to was that her sister and brother would be their best man and maid of honor so neither Ford nor Dodge would feel the one left out. He assured her neither would, but she wasn't convinced and in the end he felt it was a solid plan.

Dodge fist bumped Lincoln as he stood between he and Ford. Savannah and Logan came next down aisle. The girls were all lovely in their deep gray dresses. Savannah was beautiful but, in his opinion, no comparison to Skye. If they had children, they'd be gorgeous for certain.

Logan came to stand next to Lincoln shaking Ford and Dodge's hands then his. He winked and whispered, "This should be good."

The music grew louder and the congregation stood as The Wedding March began playing. His bride was a vision, she always was, but today she was more so. The white lace dress fit her perfectly and the crystal crown his mom and Josie gave her looked as if it was made just for her. She looked stiff and nervous as her small strides moved her toward him, but when their eyes locked he almost heard angels sing. The smile she shined on him was everything and so much more than he dreamed. His heart hammered in his chest and he concentrated to keep his breathing regular and shallow. Right now what he needed more than anything else was to hold her in his arms.

Her father had been working out and practicing walking without a walker or cane; he decided he could make it down the aisle without any help. He was doing amazingly well. Melissa wiped her eyes and dabbed at her nose with a tissue which made him grin. When they stopped at the front of the alter, Jeff shook Lincoln's hand, kissed his daughter on the cheek, and stepped around her dress slowly, making his way to the pew next to Melissa.

Lincoln held out his hand to Skye and the instant she took it, his heart raced. She turned to face him, her observant eyes searching his face for signs that something was amiss. Josie had told him Skye felt that something was wrong. The Pastor began, "You may be seated. Lincoln and Skye, please step forward."

Stepping up on the altar, his movements weren't as agile as he'd hoped they would be and she looked him in the eye. "Are you alright?"

"I am now. I will be. We will be."

Biting her bottom lip, the Pastor began a recitation and he felt good to have the reprieve before the ass chewing he knew he'd take soon enough.

37

CAN WE COME OUT NOW?

"You may kiss your bride." The instant she put her arms around him, he winced, then tried to cover it up. She could feel the tightness of bandages under his tuxedo, but before she could say anything his lips touched hers. His arms tightened around her waist and her eyes closed. She loved the way he kissed her. His tongue swept into her mouth briefly and the congregation cheered. When they pulled away from each other, she could feel the blush heat her chest and cheeks. The Pastor announced, "Ladies and Gentlemen allow me to introduce you to Mr. and Mrs. Lincoln Winter."

The congregation stood, the music began, Lincoln took her hand in his, and stepped off the altar helping her step around her train as he did. She saw the wince on his handsome face again and decided his time was almost up for 'fessing up' to whatever had happened this morning. Then she'd take her mother's advice, but not until he confessed.

They walked down the aisle to congratulations and a

smattering of applause. The smiles she received from family and friends made her feel positively giddy.

Walking through the doors at the back of the church, she stopped to chat with the door usher. "Please give us a couple of minutes before letting everyone out."

He nodded, glanced at Lincoln, then back to her, but said nothing. Exiting the church into the vestibule, she stopped and turned her new husband to face her. "Lincoln, I love you. I wouldn't have married you if I didn't. But I want to know what's been going on. And don't tell me nothing."

She held his hands in hers and forced him to look at her. He cleared his throat. "I was attacked from behind, fell down the mountain a few feet, and broke two ribs."

He looked deeply into her eyes waiting for a response from her but continued, "I'm sorry. I promised I wouldn't come to the wedding all beat up and I didn't mean to. I just thought maybe we had a shot and stopping Mangus Santarino and his goons. I only want you safe, Princess. That's what I want more than anything else."

Well, how could you be mad at him for that? She swallowed and blinked furiously to keep the tears in check. "Okay. Thank you for telling me. Thank you for wanting to keep me safe."

She could tell he was surprised, his head snapped back slightly, and his brows rose into his hairline. The most handsome man she'd ever laid eyes on definitely.

He bent his knees so they were eye level. "I love you, Skye Winter." Then his lips parted in the biggest smile she'd seen on him. "That sounds wonderful. Skye Winter."

The door opened and Logan poked his head out. "Can we come out now?"

She giggled, kissed her husband, then answered, "Yes."

***

Keep reading for a sneak peek at Dodge: Finding His Jewel

Dodge Sager entered the Copper Cup, his favorite hangout, highly alert and ready for action. Not his usual action, but work action. He was itching to find Mangus Santarino and follow him to his hiding place. He had an enormous gleaming pink diamond to retrieve from Mangus, the damned thief. Big Three Bounty Hunting's client, Guardwell, wanted the diamond back before its client raised all sorts of holy hell about it. That would ruin its reputation as being the only security transport company to never have anything stolen from them.

Glancing around he noted briefly the smattering of people in the bar. It wouldn't get busy till later which is probably why his informant told him Mangus would be here early. Taking a seat at the bar, the bartender, who was also his friend, Derek, jerked his head to the right but kept on wiping the bar down. "Usual?"

"Yeah." His eyes traveled in the direction of Derek's nod. In the back of the bar, where the booths were lined up along the wall for diners, sat a man wearing a baseball cap that boasted "Dodgers." Derek set his drink, which in reality was tea poured in a bourbon glass, in front of him on a napkin. Dodge met Derek's gaze and listened as his friend said, "Back booth, baseball cap, sexy brunette with him."

Lifting his drink to his lips, his eyes sought out the brunette with Mangus. Since Mangus was a married man, and this was not his wife according to the photographs he'd seen, he wondered what this was all about.

The dark haired beauty threw her head back and laughed and Dodge was mesmerized by the sound. Damn woman had no idea what she was getting herself into.

Derek came back around after delivering drinks to other customers and laid a menu on the bar.

"Did the brunette come in with him?"

"Nope, she was here by herself. Began shooting pool with those guys in the back, kicked their asses, and then made her way back to your friend."

Women! It was difficult to trust them in the best of circumstances. He'd learned that a long time ago.

The brunette stood from the booth and jutted her spectacular breasts out which not only got Mangus' attention but his too. He may not trust women, but he sure did love to look, touch, and feel them. She picked up Mangus' glass and sauntered her sexy ass to the bar.

His eyes darted to Mangus and noted that he watched her ass as she walked away from him. Then he locked eyes with her. Dark shiny eyes pierced his. Her long dark lashes perfectly framed her almond shaped eyes and her full pink lips curved up slightly.

She set both hers and Mangus' glasses on the bar and purred, "Refill please."

She turned her head, her dark hair held hints of auburn and shined under the lights above the bar. "Mama, you have no idea what you're getting into with that man over there."

She laughed, then glared at him, which made the hair on the back of his neck stand, "Baby, you have no idea who I am or what I'm capable of."

Something plummeted into the bottom of his stomach at her look and the tone of her voice. Alarm bells rang in his head, then she interrupted his dark thoughts. "Mind your own business, Tarzan."

Derek set her drinks on the wooden bar top. She reached into her back pocket, pulled out a twenty-dollar bill, and handed it to him. "Keep it, I'll be back for more." She picked up her drinks, and without another glance in Dodge's direction her sexy ass moved away from him and back to Mangus.

Derek's chuckle caught his attention, the stupid dimple in his cheek that the women swooned over practically pointed at him and mocked him. "Man, she burned you good."

"She didn't burn me."

Derek laughed out loud then. "She so did, bro."

He walked to the other end of the bar to tend to customers leaving the view open to watch Mangus and the hot little mama with the sassy mouth.

Having Derek refill his "tea", he continued to look like a bored patron and tried not to stare at Mangus and his date. Suddenly, Mangus reached across the table and grabbed a handful of her gorgeous hair jerking her head back. He leaned forward and said something to her, jerked again on her hair, then released her. He sat back, the snarl on his face disgusting. The hot little mama frowned, then quick as the flip of a switch she smiled.

Dodge stood and made his way to the back of the bar and to Mangus. She didn't know what she was getting into. "That is no way to treat a lady."

The slow deliberate turn of Mangus' head almost turned his stomach. This was not a man who was used to being told what to do. "That so?" The question hung in the air like a thick cloud.

Get Dodge: Finding His Jewel here.

Keep in touch and learn about new releases, sales, recipes, and other fun things by signing up for my newsletter - https://www.subscribepage.com/PJsReadersClub_copy

ALSO BY PJ FIALA

Click here to see a list of all of my books with the blurbs.

Contemporary Romance

Rolling Thunder Series

Moving to Love, Book 1

Moving to Hope, Book 2

Moving to Forever, Book 3

Moving to Desire, Book 4

Moving to You, Book 5

Moving Home, Book 6

Moving On, Book 7

Second Chances Series

Designing Samantha's Love, Book 1

Securing Kiera's Love, Book 2

Military Romantic Suspense

Bluegrass Security Series

Heart Thief, Book One

Finish Line, Book Two

Lethal Love, Book Three

Big 3 Security

Ford: Finding His Fire Book One

Lincoln: Finding His Mark Book Two

Dodge: Finding His Jewel Book Three

Rory: Finding His Match Book Four

GHOST

Defending Keirnan, GHOST Book One

Defending Sophie, GHOST Book Two

Defending Roxanne, GHOST Book Three

Defending Yvette, GHOST Book Four

Defending Bridget, GHOST Book Five

Defending Isabella, GHOST Book Six

RAPTOR

Saving Shelby, RAPTOR Book One

DEAR READER

Thank you so much for reading Lincoln, Bounty Hunters Book Two. Did you know that when you rate a book with only stars and no text the author does not see it? It also doesn't help us with vendor ratings either. But, by simply writing five words or more, this greatly helps us out so we can apply for promotions to further market our books. Would you please consider a few words along with your star rating? I thank you in advance and hope to see you on the internet.

Also, if you like to stay informed of all things related to my books, or love the chance to win a book from my author friends, join my reader's club, it's free and easy to do, just click on Readers Club below. Thank you.

PJ's Readers' Club

FOLLOW PJ

Follow me!

PJ's website

PJ's Road Queens

PJ's Readers' Club

PJ on Facebook

Instagram

Amazon

Bookbub

See inspiration photos on Pinterest

MEET PJ

I was born in a suburb of St. Louis, Missouri named Bridgeton. During my time in Missouri, I explored the Ozarks, swam in the Mississippi River, and played kickball and endless games of hide-and-seek with the neighborhood kids. The summers spent in Kentucky with my grandmother, Ruth, are the fondest childhood memories for me.

At the age of thirteen, my family moved to Wisconsin to learn to farm. Yes, learn to farm! That was interesting. Taking city kids and throwing them on a farm with twenty-eight cows purchased from the Humane Society because they had been abused was a learning experience. I learned to milk cows, the ins and outs of breeding and feeding schedules, the never-ending haying in the summer and trying to stay warm in the winter. Our first winter in Wisconsin, one storm brought 36 inches of snow, and we were snowed in for three days! Needless to say, I didn't love Wisconsin.

I'm now married with four children and four grandchildren. I have learned to love Wisconsin, though I still hate snow. My husband and I travel around by motorcycle seeing new sites and meeting new people. It never ceases to amaze me how many people are interested in where we're going and what we've seen along the way. At every gas station, restaurant, and hotel, people come up to us and ask us about what we're doing, as well as offer advice on which roads in the area are better than others.

I come from a family of veterans, my grandfather, father, brother, two of my sons, and one daughter-in-law are all veterans. Needless to say, I'm proud to be an American and proud of the service my amazing family has given.